PRAISE FOR *LIFE IS FUNNY*

★ "... an uplifting book about resilience, loyalty, and courage."—*Publishers Weekly*, starred review

★ "First novelist Frank breaks new ground. ...
Each chapter, each vignette within a chapter, builds
to its own climax, and the stories weave together
to surprise you."—*Booklist*, starred review

◆ "Those who embark upon this intriguing mosaic
will come away rewarded and inspired by the strength and
fortitude of its characters. An astounding first effort."
—*Kirkus Reviews*, pointer review

"Skillfully and compassionately wrought."
—*School Library Journal*

WINNER OF THE *TEEN PEOPLE* BOOK CLUB NEXT AWARD
AN ALA QUICK PICK
A YALSA 100 BEST OF THE BEST FOR THE 21ST CENTURY
A NEW YORK PUBLIC LIBRARY BEST BOOK FOR THE TEEN AGE

Also by E. R. Frank

America

Friction

Wrecked

Dime

Life Is Funny
E. R. FRANK

Atheneum Books for Young Readers
NEW YORK   LONDON   TORONTO   SYDNEY   NEW DELHI

This book is dedicated to my parents,
Amy and Bill,
whose love and pride mean the world to me,
to my sister and brother,
Claire and Jim,
who are a part of me,

and to my beloved and loving
Stephen,
who wouldn't let me quit.

atheneum

An imprint of Simon & Schuster Children's Publishing Division • 1230 Avenue of the Americas, New York, New York 10020 • This book is a work of fiction. Any references to historical events, real people, or real places are used fictitiously. Other names, characters, places, and events are products of the author's imagination, and any resemblance to actual events or places or persons, living or dead, is entirely coincidental. • Text copyright © 2000 by E. R. Frank • Cover illustration copyright © 2016 by Neil Swaab • All rights reserved, including the right of reproduction in whole or in part in any form. • Atheneum logo is a trademark of Simon & Schuster, Inc. • For information about special discounts for bulk purchases, please contact Simon & Schuster Special Sales at 1-866-506-1949 or business@simonandschuster.com. • The Simon & Schuster Speakers Bureau can bring authors to your live event. For more information or to book an event, contact the Simon & Schuster Speakers Bureau at 1-866-248-3049 or visit our website at www.simonspeakers.com. • Also available in an Atheneum hardcover edition Interior design by Mike Rosamilia; cover and hand-lettering by Russell Gordon • The text for this book is set in Hoefler. • Manufactured in the United States of America First Atheneum paperback edition May 2016 • 10 9 8 7 6 5 4 3 2 1 • The Library of Congress has cataloged the hardcover edition as follows: • Names: Frank, E. R., author. • Title: Life is funny / E.R. Frank. • Description: First Atheneum Books for Young Readers Hardcover Edition. | New York : Atheneum Books for Young Readers, [2016] | ?2000 | Summary: The lives of eleven teens of different races, economic backgrounds, and family situations living in Brooklyn, New York, become intertwined over a seven year period. • Identifiers: LCCN 2015025466 • ISBN 978-1-4814-3164-4 (hc) • ISBN 978-1-4814-3163-7 (pbk) • ISBN 978-1-4814-3165-1 (eBook) • Subjects: | CYAC: Interpersonal relations—Fiction. | Family problems—Fiction. | BISAC: JUVENILE FICTION / Social Issues / General (see also headings under Family). | JUVENILE FICTION / Social Issues / Friendship. | JUVENILE FICTION / Social Issues / Adolescence. • Classification: LCC PZ7.F84913 Li 2016 | DDC [Fic]—dc23 • LC record available at http://lccn.loc.gov/2015025466

ACKNOWLEDGMENTS

The author gratefully acknowledges and warmly thanks:

Shirley Cohen, Charlotte Davenport, Frances McClenney, and Linda Verdery for being tremendous first teachers who nurtured my love of reading and writing.

Ida Dupont, Kathy Farrow, Debbie Lefkovic-Abrams, Stacy Liss, Seema Mohanty, and Victoria Reese for their sustaining encouragement and friendship.

Stephen Lucas for confidently predicting all with perfect accuracy and for insisting on what was special in the very first draft.

Kerry Garfinkel and Jessica Kalb Roland for giving generously of their enthusiasm and editorial talent.

Mary Beth Caschetta and Karin Cook for so graciously sharing and showing the ropes.

Marcia Golub for her support and lessons in The Storyteller's Voice.

Bunny Gabel for her spirit, smart feedback, and Workshop in Writing for Children.

The 1997/1998 members of Bunny Gabel's Workshop in Writing for Children for their astute comments and kind delivery.

Jamie Callan and Frank Bergon for their years of long-distance guidance and mentoring.

The Blue Mountain Center and the Virginia Center for Creative Arts for the opportunity to write in a beautiful community with limitless cookies.

Charlotte Sheedy for taking me on, making it happen, and doing what she does so well.

Richard Jackson for these very pages and for his expertise, wit, and warmth.

And especially my grandparents: Gerold Frank for being the first inspiration and Lillian Frank for her wisdom, dignity, and humor.

Year One

China

Ebony

Grace

Eric

Keisha

Mattie

Elaine

Mickey

Tory

Keisha

Gingerbread

Sonia

Eric

DeShawn

Mara

Carl

Nick

Tory

China

AT FIRST EBONY and I don't want to, but then her mom, Ms. Giles, says she'll pay us, and we say okay because Ebony's twin sisters' day care isn't that far, plus it's across the street from McDonald's.

We wait in the playground tire swings, sipping Cokes and dipping nuggets in hot sauce, and I'm wishing I'd asked for sweet and sour, when we see him. I'm guessing he's younger than us, but he's way bigger, and he's real dark, and he doesn't look around or anything. His eyes are set straight ahead, and he walks right by and up to the front-door stoop and just stands there, waiting.

"We're fine, thank you. And what's up to you, too?" Ebony goes, loud, so he'll hear. Only he acts like he's deaf or something.

Ebony sucks her teeth for a minute, and then she tells me,

"He'd be fine if he was dressed half decent." It's hard to know if she truly cares about stuff like that or if she's just trying to get me aggravated, for fun.

So I tell her, "You'd be fine if you weren't a bitch."

"Shut up."

"You know it's true." Ebony fakes a sulk, and I check him out again.

"He wouldn't be fine anyway," I go. "He's scary."

"What do you mean?"

"Look."

She sticks her foot way out and leans way over to pretend-tie her shoe.

"You're right," she says. "He's mad scary."

A bell rings, and the doors open. A bunch of little kids shoot through, and me and Ebony hop up out of the swings. A couple of day care ladies laze out behind the kids, and that boy crosses his arms and leans his back to the brick.

Ebony's twin sisters, Mattie and Elaine, bounce outside, holding some kind of Popsicle stick craziness.

"What's that?" Ebony asks them.

"A dollhouse," Mattie says.

"It's not done," Elaine says. "We have to make the roof."

"Hi, China," Mattie says.

"Hi, baby," I go.

"Hi, China," Elaine says.

"Hey, baby," I tell her.

They're six but like it when I call them baby. Ebony's not allowed. They get mad at her when she does it. They let me because I don't have any little sisters, and I talk to them when Ebony just thinks they're around to get on her last nerve. They would let our other best friend, Grace, because she's white and she's prettier than anything, only Grace would never say baby anyway.

"China, look," Ebony goes, poking me.

One of the day care ladies is staring, pole up her butt, at that boy. "Can I help you?" she asks, nasty.

The boy stares back at her. He doesn't say a mad word.

"Do you need something?" the lady goes, like he better not.

He keeps his face shut tight, and the lady opens up her mouth again, but then this real small kid—way younger than the twins—zooms out with this Popsicle stick thing and goes to the scary boy, "Mama sick?"

The scary boy gives the lady a big old cold eye and then scoops up the real small kid and flips him over his shoulder and takes off. The kid giggles like crazy.

"Eric!" he squawks. "Eric! Let me go!"

"Bye, Mickey," Mattie yells at the small kid's upside-down giggly head.

"Bye, Mickey," Elaine yells.

"Bye, y'all!" he calls back.

But that boy Eric, he doesn't smile or slow down or anything.

On the first Friday the twins get to color mad bunches of yellow balloons with Magic Markers, and they let me and Ebony carry the balloons home. When Ebony's mom gets back from showing apartments, she taps at the bunches, making them nod and shiver all over their living room, and she goes, "'In Just-spring when the world is mud-luscious the little lame balloonman whistles far and wee and eddieandbill come running from marbles and piracies and it's spring when the world is puddle-wonderful.'"

"It's not spring," Ebony cuts in. "It's summer."

Ms. Giles leaves the balloons and the poem and digs into her pocketbook. I wanted to hear the end, but Ebony hates it when her mother says poetry. She's always making her mom stop in the middle like that.

"Thank you, girls," Ms. Giles goes, and she hands us each a fresh green bill, stiff as a new bookmark. Ebony holds hers by the edges, pushes them forward, and then pulls them back to make a loud snap. I fold a box out of mine, then undo it flat again and snap it, like Ebony.

"What's the rest of that poem?" I ask Ms. Giles.

"Ugh," Ebony moans.

"*Ugh* right back," I go.

"Be patient with her, China," her mother tells me. "Ebony's poetry hasn't bubbled up to the top yet."

That makes me picture the fish tank at school.

"Mom!" Ebony moans again.

Her mother touches my chin with her fingertips. "China," she goes, "your poetry is closer to the surface, just under your skin."

Ebony drags me to her room and then calls Grace so the two of them can tease me stupid.

"*Under her skin!*" Grace goes, all sarcastic. Ebony's got her on speaker phone.

"Y'all just wait," I tell them both.

At Grace's I work on mini-collages from old magazines, to fit into flat plastic key chains, while Grace and Ebony rip the hems out of the bottoms of their jeans. You have to do both projects just right, or you mess things all up.

"Make sure you don't get glue on the floor," Grace reminds me for the millionth time. I don't get an attitude, though, because of her mother. We're not even supposed to be at Grace's because her mom's sort of mean and doesn't like people who aren't white.

I met Ms. Sanborn once on the sidewalk, and she was kind of nasty to me and Ebony both, but it was hard to tell if it was because we're black or what, because she was mean to Grace, too, and Grace is white, plus she's her mother's own daughter.

"Y'all want to sleep over this Friday?" Ebony asks, right when I get done cutting out the words *hip* and *sex*.

"Yeah," I go, spotting *ultra* and *fine* and *Wow* all on one page. "Can you come, Grace?"

"Depends what mood her mom's in," Ebony says quick, so Grace won't have to.

Grace rolls her eyes, which she is real good at, especially for a white girl.

"Word," she goes, just to make us laugh.

That boy, Eric, stares right past us again and waits with his back to the day care wall. This time Ebony keeps her mouth shut about him, and I try to catch his eye, but he won't see me. The day care lady doesn't say anything. She looks at him like he stinks or something, and he acts like she's a speck of bug doo under his shoe.

Another girl shows up waiting today, too. She's younger than us, like that Eric boy, only she looks it more than he does because she's real small and skinny.

"Hi," she goes when she has to pass us at the tire swings.

"Hi," we go.

She sort of stops near us when she notices that Eric taking up the stoop by the day care door. Nobody knows what to say for a minute, so we all stare at him until Ebony finally goes, "You know him?"

"He switched to special ed last year," the girl says. "He fights."

"Figures." Ebony smirks. The girl kind of shrugs, while I kick at Ebony's tire. "Isn't he ugly?" Ebony goes to her, kicking my tire back.

Then the doors swing open, and the kids spill out. A real small girl, the same size as that little Mickey, skips over to us, all excited.

"Keisha!" this real small girl squeaks. "We made cookies!"

"You make some for your mama and Nick?" this Keisha asks her, all calm and still, like she's grown or something. The small girl's face goes guilty. Keisha rolls her eyes at us. "See you," she says, and they take off.

Little Mickey shows up right after that, and he grabs Eric's hand and then hums a little while they walk down the stoop and away. Like he knows underneath that hard face, Eric's smiling down at him.

"You sure you don't want to take some day classes in arts and crafts or karate?" my mom asks, over the TV.

9

"Uh huh," I tell her.

"Deadline's next week," she reminds me.

"I just want to hang out this summer."

"Twelve-year-old girls ought to keep busy," my daddy says to me. Then, to the TV, he goes, "What is the Suez Canal?" He knows every *Jeopardy* answer. The only one I ever saw him miss was "What is sulfur?"

"I keep busy," I tell him. "Grace and Ebony and me do stuff on our own."

"China's getting a little pay each week to help Ebony watch the twins on their way home from day care," my mom tells him.

"You're putting it all in the bank, right?" he goes.

"Wrong," I say, and he tries to swat my behind, but I get away, because he never for real tries to get me, plus I'm fast.

Grace and Ebony don't have daddies. Grace thinks her mother doesn't even know who he is. Ebony's lives somewhere in the South, and she hasn't seen him since she was five. Ebony's mother won't talk about him except to say that he loves Ebony but isn't enough of a man to know how to show it. They think my daddy's mad cool partly because he's got these slanty eyes like me, plus he's got a pierced ear, plus he's real nice.

"Have you ever visited him at work?" Ebony's asking me. She's pulling at the let-out hem of her jeans, to make fringes.

She does stuff slower than Grace, who's putting her jeans on to see if her done fringes are even enough.

"Once," I say. I'm busy gluing all my cutout words onto three different pieces of small cardboard. When I'm done, each collage will slip into a plastic key chain frame just like a picture would.

"Did you meet a lot of stars?"

"There's not really any stars on the news," I answer. "But he's going to switch over to a soap opera soon."

"I bet stars don't even talk to the cameramen anyway," Grace says, and then we hear the front door bang open and Grace's mother yell, "I'm home!"

"Shit," Grace goes, and the next minute her mother's standing in the bedroom doorway, hands on her hips, mouth wide enough to catch a truckload of flies.

"Hi, Ms. Sanborn," I go, to show her how polite black girls can be.

"Hi, Ms. Sanborn," Ebony goes.

"That's Ebony, and that's China," Grace says. She looks real calm, but I can see a vein, or something, bouncing in her neck.

"Nice to meet you," Grace's mom says. But she's not looking at us, plus she met us once already. I guess she doesn't remember. "Now you'll have to leave."

* * *

"What a bitch," Ebony says while we're waiting for the day care to let out. We bought McDonald's again, but we're too mad to eat.

"You think she'll let Grace sleep over with us Friday?"

"You think she's going to shit honey anytime soon?"

"Hey," I go. "That boy isn't around. That Eric boy."

"What. You like him now?" Ebony starts smirking.

"It's not like that," I go.

"Riiight," she says, all attitude.

"For real," I tell her.

The bell rings, and the twins run out. They're wearing all kinds of painted and strung-up macaroni. Bracelets, necklaces, belts.

"Y'all want some nuggets?" we ask. They grab them and run off to the jungle gym.

I see that Mickey looking around. I see him walk to the playground's fence. I see him stare over at a lady I didn't notice before who's leaning on the fence gate. She's way skinny and ashy like you never saw. Mickey scuffs over to her. She starts walking away as soon as he's near. He speeds up to get next to her and hands over his macaroni necklace. She puts it on over her head, without stopping or even looking at him or anything.

Today he's not giggling. Or humming.

*   *   *

"May I speak to Grace, please?" I go.

"No, you may not," her mom says. "Grace is grounded from the phone."

"I'm sorry we didn't have your permission," I say. I don't want to get Grace into more mess, but still.

"Your apology is accepted."

"We're real clean," I say. "And we don't make any noise or bother your neighbors."

"I'll tell Grace you called," Ms. Sanborn says.

"Grace is our best friend," I tell her.

"I'm aware of that."

"Maybe you could ask our mothers to punish us instead," I say. "Because, really, we kind of made Grace let us come over."

"Good-bye," her mom says. Then she hangs up the phone.

What a bitch.

On Thursday me and Ebony don't hang out together at Grace's first, so we meet up at the day care. I get there early. That younger girl, Keisha, is hanging out by the tire swings. Eric's leaning up against the wall. I wave to Keisha and then walk up the stoop to Eric.

"Hi," I go. He doesn't say anything. Plus he does kind of smell.

"You want a nugget?" I ask. He glares at the nuggets, and then he glares at me.

"I saw your mother yesterday," I go.

He won't say a mad word. Maybe it wasn't even his mother.

"Is she sick?"

"Get the fuck out my face," he tells me.

Friday Grace races into the McDonald's right when me and Ebony are ordering.

"Hey, girl!" Ebony goes. "How'd you get out?"

"I'm grounded for a month, same for the phone," Grace pants. "But my mom's at work every day. So screw her." She's red and shiny from running in the heat. All the McDonald's boys are staring at her under their baseball hats. She plays like she doesn't notice, though.

"My mom's not paying you," Ebony warns.

"Like I want your money," Grace says.

"Oooooh," I go.

Outside we see Eric walking ahead of us.

"That's him," Ebony tells Grace. "That's the one China wants to get with. Isn't he nasty?"

"I do not either want to get with him," I say. "And don't call him nasty. Something's wrong with his mother or something."

"So?" Ebony goes. "He's still nasty."

The thing I notice today just about knocks me over. You'd think he'd slide his eyes over Grace if he slid them over anybody. But it's like he doesn't even see her. The person he watches is Ebony when she stoops in the middle of the playground to help Mattie reglue her milk carton castle.

Grace's mother has a date with some new neighbor, so Grace sneaks out to Ebony's.

"Somebody would get with your mom?" Ebony goes, and then she says quick, "No offense."

"Like I care," Grace tells us. We're in the kitchen, making brownies. When we're at Ebony's, we bake. At my house it's usually popcorn. We don't eat at Grace's.

"You girls want a movie?" Ebony's mother asks, poking her head into the kitchen.

The phone rings, and Ebony grabs it. "Hello," she goes.

"That's the twins," her mom tells us. They're at an overnight somewhere.

"This is Ebony," Ebony says. Then she gets real quiet. I guess it's not the twins.

"Who is it?" Ms. Giles asks.

"Uh huh," Ebony goes.

"Ebony?"

"I don't remember," Ebony tells the phone. "I didn't get

any." Then she says, "Hang on." She holds out the phone.

"He says he's my daddy," she goes. "He's crying."

Ms. Giles grabs the phone and covers the receiver with her hand.

"Go upstairs," she orders us. "Now."

We stretch across Ebony's bed and try to figure out how to listen in, but even though Ebony's got mad phone stuff, like call waiting and speaker and three way, we can't figure out anything for spying.

"What did he sound like?" Grace asks.

"He was all happy at first," Ebony goes. "He was real happy." She's swinging around her sock monkey doll by his tail.

"He was all how he sent me these letters on my birthdays, and did I like them."

"You never told us about any letters," Grace says.

"Well, I never got any, girl," Ebony goes, popping Grace's knee with that monkey.

"You said he was crying," I say.

"He was."

"But you said he was happy."

"He was crying from happiness," Grace guesses, rolling her eyes.

"Wrong," Ebony says. "He was crying when I told him I never got any dumbass letters."

We all think about that for a minute, trying to figure it out, and then Grace asks me, "Did you ever see your dad cry?"

"Nope."

"Did y'all ever see your mothers cry?" Ebony goes.

We shake our heads, and then Ebony's mom walks in.

"Was that really my daddy?" Ebony asks. She doesn't sit up or anything. She just keeps swinging that sock monkey over her head.

"Yes," her mom says. "Do you want to talk about this now, with your friends here?" she goes. "Or do you want to wait until you and I can discuss it on our own?"

Ebony shrugs. Me and Grace look at each other. I know she's hoping what I am. We want to hear all about it.

"Maybe we should wait until tomorrow then," Ms. Giles says.

Ebony shrugs again.

Grace sneaks home an hour later, and I wake up in the middle of the night without Ebony next to me. I get spooked, but when I find Ebony all tucked in with her mother, I step away because it seems like something private.

"'. . . and how you first fluttered,'" I hear Ebony's mom whispering, "'then jumped and I thought it was my heart.'"

At the tire swings Ebony chomps at her nails and spits the bits out in a pile.

"That's disgusting," Grace tells her.

Ebony's daddy called again yesterday. Her mom doesn't know. Ebony said he was telling her all about some woman he wants her to meet. Ebony said he was talking slow and sounded like he was forgetting words a lot of the time. Grace said maybe he'd been drinking.

"Y'all want to sleep over at my house on Friday?" I go, while I'm looking at Eric, trying to figure out what that mad bulge is in his back pocket.

"Mmmkay," Ebony says.

"I'll come by for a while," Grace goes. She'll have to sneak out again. She's still got a week left on punishment.

Ebony squints over at Eric. "He stinks," she tells me, evil. "I can smell him from here." That's a lie.

"It's not his fault," I go.

"How do you know?" Grace says, not evil, only curious.

"I just do."

"You're the one who said he was scary," Ebony tells me, standing up from the swings.

"I changed my mind," I say. "And stop talking loud. He's not deaf."

"So?"

"Hi, girls," we hear, and Ebony's mother comes through the gate.

"Do we still get paid for today?" Ebony asks when her mom gets to our swings.

"Of course," Ms. Giles says. "I can't stay anyway. I'm on my way to Fifth Street to show a two-bedroom."

I'm trying to catch Eric's eye, but he's stupid stubborn. I guess Ebony's mother sees me looking. "Who's that?" she asks.

"Some fool," Ebony says.

"He's not a fool," I tell them.

"He kind of is," Grace says.

"He is not!" I go, loud.

"What's your problem?" Ebony snaps, and then Grace, instead of rolling her eyes at me, she sucks her teeth hard at Ebony and kicks near the fingernail pile.

"He's not a fool," I tell Ebony's mother. My voice is crazy shaky, and my face is all hot, and I don't even know why.

Ms. Giles puts her hand on my shoulder and looks over at Eric. I try to keep from crying while the bell rings and the kids fly through the doors. Ebony's mother watches the day care lady glare at Eric until Mickey comes out, his nose all nasty. Eric yanks a tissue from his back pocket bulge and holds it up to Mickey's face.

"Blow," he goes.

"Battered by the tides like an abandoned ship, a spirit adrift," Ms. Giles says, real low.

"Mom!" Ebony groans at her.

"Just chill," Grace snaps at Ebony. "Jesus."

"He's got poetry," I go, all choky. "He's got mad poetry."

I get a runny head and start feeling wobbly, and my mom takes my temperature and then kicks my daddy off the couch during *Jeopardy* so I can lie down. My daddy gives me the clicker and sits in the armchair, and my mom puts the tissue box and a blanket, even though it's about a million degrees outside, on the coffee table. Then she brings me this special kind of aspirin she gets for free from her boss at the drugstore and lemon honey tea and tells me to drink it hot. My daddy feels my forehead and the fat mug with the back of his hand and then makes my mom drop ice cubes into the tea, to cool it.

"You're going to kill her," he scolds. "She's going to melt like the Wicked Witch of the West."

Then they sit with me watching whatever I want to for

a while, and right in the middle of a car commercial I understand "a spirit adrift," and I feel this thing ease through my
skin with the fever, showing me how mad stupid mean the
world can be and just how lucky I got, and it's a warm sad feeling, like tea steam wrapping comfort around some new, crying
part of my heart.

Keisha

OKAY. WHAT HAPPENED was, at the end of last year
Mara was best friends with Jessie, but then Mara's boyfriend,
who's in high school now, fooled around with Jessie. So Mara
beat up Jessie, and then Jessie and this girl Trisha were best
friends, and me and Mara and this other Jessie were best
friends. But then this Jessie number two moved to Queens
and Jessie number one beat up Mara on the first day of school
this year for beating her up last year, and then she and Mara
were best friends again, and Trisha ended up being best
friends with some girl from California.

So then Mara started going out with this white boy, and
Jessie started going out with DeShawn. But then the white
boy got suspended for a week after he called that ugly special
ed Eric kid "welfare chickenhead can't read chicken feed" and

the Eric kid threw a chair at the white boy, and the white boy threw a chair back, and it hit this hyper round-face Gingerbread boy in the back of the head, and the white boy and ugly special ed Eric both got suspended, and then DeShawn wouldn't talk to Mara even though she wasn't any part of it, and then Mara told Jessie if she hung with DeShawn, they couldn't be friends. So Jessie dumped DeShawn at lunch, and DeShawn said he was going out with JaNeesha anyway, which wasn't true because I used to be friends with JaNeesha and she never even liked him.

Okay. So when we had the food map project for history class, Mara and Jessie and me were all in the same group and they let me be their second best friend, so ever since Thanksgiving we've all three been mad tight, and we're all going to the same high school one day and then later go out with NBA players and live near a park and travel to Disney World every summer. We're all going to end up the same except Mara's going to stay darker than me, and I'm going to stay darker than Jessie, and also Mara wants three girls and three boys, and Jessie only wants boys, and I don't want either because when I get old, I'm just going to keep my aunt Eva and my little cousin Tory for family the same way Aunt Eva keeps me and my brother, Nick, right now.

So anyway, what happens is me and Mara and Jessie are

in the girls' bathroom before the lunch bell when JaNeesha comes out of the last stall, and she gets up in Jessie's face. She goes, "That's mines." She's talking about Jessie's beeper, which Jessie got for her birthday two weeks ago from her grandma. So anyway, JaNeesha's kind of small, but she's strong and everybody knows it ever since last year she beat up some boy who got transferred for pinching her tit, which she didn't even really have tits yet.

"You bugging," Jessie says. Usually she talks more like me, with more white English and all because her grandma is kind of like my aunt Eva about that, but when somebody's in your face, it's better to talk normal. So anyway, I can tell she's crazy scared because she's real small and not too strong, which everybody knows, even though she fights hard.

The thing is, you're supposed to take your friend's back if they get jumped. But JaNeesha used to be my friend, too, and we never had a fight, and I'm not real sure what I'm supposed to do: take Jessie's back against JaNeesha's or JaNeesha's back against Jessie's. I think I'm supposed to take Jessie's back since we're the best friends right now. But then Mara does a real kind friend thing because she gets close to me and goes, quiet so nobody else can hear, "I got her back if you got to check out."

But I stay where I am because maybe it won't get like that anyway, and I want to see what's going to happen.

So JaNeesha goes, "That's mines, motherfucker."

And she grabs for Jessie's beeper, and Jessie jumps up mad quick right on the sink so she's way taller then the rest of us, and she goes, "What you got to start with me for, bitch! That ain't your beeper, and you ain't getting nothing till I shove it up your behind!"

JaNeesha plays like she's going to crash Jessie in the knees and right off that sink, but Jessie kicks out real hard, and the next thing you know, JaNeesha's teeth are all over the floor, and now Jessie won't have to worry about people starting with her anymore.

Then JaNeesha looks at me with crazy blood pouring out of her mouth and tries to yell something, but she kind of can't, I guess because it hurts and she's missing all these teeth, and then here comes Ms. Lyons, screaming, and if it weren't for Jessie looking so scared up there on that sink and JaNeesha bleeding all over everything, I'd laugh because white people scream for the dumbest reasons and never get loud when they ought to.

So then after the principal gets through talking to everybody who saw, this eighth grader Indian girl who comes from the high school to peer-tutor Jessie and some other kids for math on Thursdays, this girl, Sonia, who stepped out of the third stall right when Jessie got up on that sink, she tells us if you don't want to see the guidance counselor on the second floor, there's some old art closet where there's a couple of chairs and some old mattress and you can stay in there if you want to be by yourself and nobody ever finds you, not even other kids if you don't want because you can lock it from the inside.

So now that's why I'm sitting here, because I have to be alone to try and figure out two things that are getting on my nerves, bad. One of them is what do I do to stay out of fights at least for the next seven years until I'm done with high school because I'm supposed to graduate and my aunt Eva will kill me if I don't, but everybody's always wanting to fight, and then you get suspended and kicked out and all that mess. And then the other thing is what do I do if I don't want my brother, Nick, to be touching me on my privacy every night and he comes and does it anyway?

Year Two

Sonia
Monique
Sam

Drew
Sonia
Gingerbread
Sam
Josh
Carl

Sonia

WHEN MY FAVORITE brother said the man who jumped off the Statue of Liberty was Sarim, I didn't believe it. Nif is honest as a reflection with me, but still. I just couldn't picture Sarim up there, on that stone pedestal underneath Liberty's toes, floating along balloonlike in that peaceful way he has and then spinning out of control, popped, zigzagging up and over the edge. I couldn't believe it.

Not even after the whole neighborhood gathered in our living room, the women staying nearer to the kitchen and the men sitting on our couches closer to the television. They were all talking about Sarim, about the way his body must have looked crushed into the lower balcony's cement, the way the cement must have looked. Mostly they spoke in Hindi, the Asian tones automatically sounding more like grief to me than anything English, and I still didn't believe it was Sarim. My mother and the other women cooked all week, for the neighborhood gathered at our third-floor apartment. They gathered here because we are across the street from the brownstone building where Sarim lives. Used to live.

I believe it more now. It's been two weeks, and he hasn't come home. And my four older brothers swore it was Sarim's body they saw at the funeral before it was sent back to Pakistan to be cremated. And everyone says it was his watch and his wallet, his Bic pens and Certs and his tigereye touchstones they found, scattered near and far from the body, like coins around the center of a gory wishing well. I guess it must be him.

Even now nobody wants to use the word *suicide* because killing yourself goes against the beliefs of my religion, and everybody feels uneasy with improper behavior. Lots of things are improper for Muslims. Especially for girls. Especially in my family. Wearing shorts, cutting your hair, doing poorly in school, arguing with anyone who is older, talking to a boy or to a man who is not related to you. I've always made my parents proud of me by appearing to follow each rule perfectly. Up until Sarim, I made myself proud, too, and pleased, because when you behave properly, you know just exactly where you belong. And knowing where you belong is very comforting, like a large hand resting on the top of your head.

I'm not sure what happens after you die. I think my brothers learn about that at their school or maybe during their weekend religious classes, but not even Nif talks about those things with me. I've read enough to know that a lot of Americans don't believe in God, don't think there's anything after death. For others, there's heaven and hell, or reincarnation. I want to find out what Muslims believe, what I'm supposed to believe, but the person I'd normally ask isn't here anymore.

I worry about what happened to him. First I worry that he's somewhere out there and can see everything that I'm doing and hear everything I'm saying. That his spirit is like eyes and ears of air. That if he thinks there are moments when I'm not missing him and thinking about him, his feelings would be hurt. Which is why I try to whisper his name at least every half an hour, why his photograph has to be admired every night in my closet, behind a stack of blankets and with Nif's pen flashlight. Why I excuse myself from every class every day at least once to pray in the girls' bathroom for him, why when I'm alone I'll speak out loud to him, hoping he will hear.

I miss you, Sarim, I hope it didn't hurt too much, Sarim, I know you're not crazy, Sarim.

I have to say his name with each new sentence so that he will know it's him I'm talking to.

Then, other times, I worry that he's nowhere. Blackness. Not even blackness. Nothingness.

Sarim moved to Brooklyn, across the street from my family, just before the school year began. The first time I spoke to him was two weeks later, on his twenty-sixth birthday, when he had a party for the whole neighborhood. He charmed all the parents and the grandparents with his quiet, small-smile face and with stories of growing up Muslim in France and then returning to Pakistan to discover an entire world of boys just like him: dark-skinned and praying five times a day. Even my mother and father let him make them laugh and told him to knock on our door anytime he might need milk, bread, or company.

After the women had swept away any sign of biscuit crumbs or crumpled napkins, after almost everyone had left with sugar stomachs and tea breath, Nif and I and three kids from the next block stayed to play one last game of hide-and-seek. I'd ducked into the front coat closet to find Sarim already there, grinning at me through thick wool sleeves and dangling knit scarves, pulling me in before I could blink. We talked for a long time before we heard my brother clomping toward us. I forgot all about the rules.

Sarim told me he was a graduate student studying law. He

told me he'd grown up in a small town near Paris, the only child of a widow. He didn't remember his father, who died in some kind of accident when Sarim was only three months old. Sarim asked me all about the eighth grade and about my family and how I felt when I left Pakistan. He talked to me as though I were an adult; he listened as though everything I said were actually important. He was the first one who made me feel like me.

On the short walk home that night, Nif pulled me back from my parents and older brothers and threatened to tell my father about the closet. I shouldn't have even talked to Sarim. Shouldn't have shut myself up inside a box with him where our legs could bump and our faces almost touched in the dark. Shame filled my throat and ears like a hot swarm of bees. If you're a part of my family, you want to be the most perfect you can be. You want your parents always to lift their heads high when they speak about you to their friends. You want always to know yourself what you do and don't deserve and where you belong. To have all of that, it's very important to follow the rules. It's important not to question your father or husband or any holy man or to ask for explanations. You must trust the wisdom of the men. You must follow their wisdom at all times. The embarrassment my parents would feel when they discovered how terribly I'd behaved would sit on our home like a wet stink. They might send me back to Pakistan.

"If it is too difficult for you to follow our laws here in this country, Hanif," my father had once said after Nif had been spotted by a neighbor sneaking out of a movie theater, "you will have to go home, where temptation is not always so near."

But when I told him he was right and that I would confess to my father immediately about the closet, Nif got nervous. It's a brother's responsibility to help a sister keep from being improper. As the one closest to me in age and in friendship, Nif knew he would be disgraced a little bit along with me. So he never told, and even with my shame, I didn't either. I meant to, but that night I noticed that I could see from my window into Sarim's. He waved at me.

Sometimes Sarim disappeared for a few days. I wouldn't spot his light blink on, wouldn't pass him in the street. I never had the courage to ask him where he went, and he never told me. But I began to know when to expect his disappearances because just before them, the circles under his eyes would be darker than usual, the small smile more fixed, and his soft, steady walk would lighten into a float.

What? he'd ask me sometimes, a lot of times, when I hadn't said anything. I always thought he was just tired, exhausted.

Law school must be very hard, I'd answer. He would nod and hand me one of his brown-and-yellow ribboned touchstones.

These make it easier, he'd say, letting me hold the smoothness for a moment. I never knew what he was talking about, really, but the feel of cool shine in my palm distracted me from asking anything more.

You're not crazy, Sarim, I whisper a lot these days. *I'm sure there's some other explanation.*

We became friends without anyone knowing. The shame faded, or maybe it hid somehow, like a virus or a cavity, and I stopped worrying that we were doing anything wrong. Even though we talked on the street when nobody was looking or spoke at neighborhood parties and festivals in a crowd that probably thought he was my cousin or uncle. Even though sometimes, on a detour home from an errand for my mother, I would visit quickly in his apartment. Fifteen minutes there, ten minutes here.

He wrote me notes and left them under his front stoop mud mat folded into hard packages, little blue-lined squares filled with slanted ink.

Dear Sonia,
    Yes, I do know how to cook, though I rarely have time to prepare my own meals.

Regarding our discussion of waves, I believe that water does not move forward so much, but rather seems to rise and fall in place.

I prefer butterscotch to licorice.

Yesterday, there was a dress in the red shade you admire in a shop window on Seventh Avenue.

Sonia, every dog does not bite, nor does each bee sting. For each schoolmate who insults you, there must be fifty who do not. And for every Muslim terrorist, there are thousands of us who oppose violence. Tell those who are cruel to you that in their cruelty, they are the terror. Then inform them that they are forgiven, for such forgiveness may shame some toward kindness.

Love,

Sarim

After a while, not even Nif knew how close Sarim and I had become. In public we had to pretend we didn't know each other very well. Pretending always made me smile inside, a special secret between Sarim and me.

So when he died, when he killed himself, I wasn't expected to cry but to marvel. To whisper with the others and watch his blanket-covered body on Channel 7. I wasn't expected to

leave the sink running until it overflowed or to lose my homework and fight with Nif. I wasn't expected to rip my fingernails bloody, to forget to shower, to lose ten pounds. Maybe
it was because these things were not expected of me that
nobody noticed them.

At school I try hard to keep my slippery feelings hidden
inside some outer hardness. I picture my skin as a brown egg-
shell hiding the slimy mess of its insides. It works until the
end of gym today, when some kids begin to guess whether
that Statue of Liberty man was dead even before he hit the
lower balcony that caught him.

"Not," says a ninth grader called Monique, who usually
skips to smoke in the locker room. Today she is caught and
made to watch the rest of us from the lowest bench of the
bleachers. "He was wide awake on the way down," she says, as
though she really knows. "Scared shitless."

My shell tears with hard little rips while this Monique
smirks and leans back on her elbows. "That asshole felt
everything when he hit. Pain like you wouldn't fucking
believe."

A boy who is not Muslim and who is not Pakistani but who
has rich skin close to the color of Sarim's brings a gym teacher
for me. I am frozen underneath the corner basketball hoop.

"Something's wrong with her," the boy says. I think his name is Sam. A name close to Sarim's. I begin to cry.

"What's the matter with you?" Ms. Manning scolds.

I can't move.

"I saw her here before lunch," the boy tells us. "She's an eighth grader."

"Before lunch?" Ms. Manning asks.

"Yeah," he says.

The guidance counselor agrees not to call my parents if I agree to visit her three times a week for an hour. Another rule broken. In Pakistan you don't share your problems with anyone outside the family. Definitely not outside the religion. The guidance counselor is Spanish and Catholic. She wears a tiny gold cross on a tiny gold chain around her neck. Improper. I'm improper. I explain that, and she nods, as if she knows. She doesn't seem to be offended.

She asks if there's anyone in my community I could share this with instead of talking to her. There's not. My parents would hear about it practically before I could even decide who to tell. The guidance counselor and I are stuck with each other. She asks if I want to kill myself, and I am so surprised I stop crying.

"Why would I want to do that?" I say, and she seems pleased.

Her office is full of bright cloth flowers and desktop toys. It smells of cinnamon.

In my dream I am screaming at Sarim's broken body, *How could you do it! How could you?* I wake up in front of my window, looking down at his. There's no light. No Sarim. He's gone, and he's taken me with him. In the bathroom mirror my face looks like his: dark circles under my eyes, distraction in my mouth.

I bring my report card to the guidance counselor. I failed every test taken in the past two and a half weeks. I have two Bs and a C. They are my first Bs and C. I've always gotten only As. My parents could send me back to Pakistan.

"It's his fault!" I wail. "It's his fault!"

"I'm not really angry," I tell her at our next meeting.

She ignores that. "Write to him," she suggests. "Tell him every feeling you have. Allow yourself only one hour each night. No more leaving class to talk to him, stop visiting his picture in the middle of the night, don't keep repeating his name all the time. Just the letter one hour each day. No more, no less. Then sleep."

I follow her directions. I write him letters and leave them in hard packages under his front stoop mud mat. I tell myself the ones I left the day before look as though they've been opened, read, and refolded. I leave them all there, letting them collect and flatten under the mat. The guidance counselor asks if I'd like to read them out loud to her. I don't bring them in, but I tell her about what I write, and we talk about all of it. I gain back five pounds and make straight As. My hair gleams like polished shoes, and I stop picking at Nif and my fingers. I'm required to see the counselor only once a week.

But it's improper. I wasn't supposed to be talking to a man. I'm not supposed to be talking to a Spanish Catholic guidance counselor. They'll find out. My older brothers will hear their friends speak disrespectfully of me. The neighborhood will whisper about it behind our backs. My mother and father will be ashamed. Muslims are competitive that way. The children must shine for the sake of the parents.

Dear Sarim,

Why did you do it? Were you feeling sad, and if so, why didn't you tell me? I would have listened. I am very angry at you for doing such a stupid thing. I am angry at you for leaving me like that. You didn't even stop to think how this would be for me. You were selfish. You disappointed me. If you ever come back, I'll kill you all over again for what you have done.

Dear Sarim,

I didn't mean what I said in the last letter. I keep thinking of you all alone, climbing. I keep wondering how much pain you must have been in to do what you did. I cry every time I think of how lonely you must have been, how upset you must have been to do something like that. I wish you could have told me what had happened. Did something happen? Did something or someone upset you? What made you do it? I just need to understand because it's very hard being here without you and not understanding why you aren't here.

Dear Sarim,

In case you can't hear the words I say to you and can only see the words written here, I want to make sure you know a few things: I love you. I miss you. You are the most special person I ever knew. Thank you for being my friend.

Dear Sarim,

Could you at least give me a sign that you've gotten all of my messages? It's very hard for me not knowing what or where you are.

I'm a disgrace. I've met with the guidance counselor too many times.

I cry each time, and she doesn't seem to mind. Each time she asks if we might call my parents to share with them what I am feeling. I won't let her. Each time she asks me how bad things are, if I might kill myself, and then, why not? We talk about death and what it means. When I refuse to be angry that I wasn't allowed to go to the funeral, that I wasn't allowed to love him, she gets angry for me. She tries not to show it, but I can tell by the way her voice changes, by the way she has trouble looking at me. At first her anger is a relief. Later it makes me sad.

"When will all this go away?" I ask her.

"In time," she says.

I used to believe that anyone who kills himself must be crazy. Now I think about what it really means to be crazy. Because Sarim wasn't. He was kind and quiet and had ideas and feelings and studied law. He made other people happy. He listened to everyone. He floated and smiled and sometimes disappeared. But he wasn't crazy.

Dear Sarim,
    Why didn't you come to me first if you were feeling so bad?

Sometimes when I'm talking to the guidance counselor, a little worm of fear crawls up through my belly and into my neck. Fear that maybe he did try to talk to me about something, and I didn't listen carefully enough. Fear that he'd asked for my help somehow, and I hadn't given it to him.

The guidance counselor guesses about the worm.

"One thing I do know," she tells me, "is that when someone we love dies, a lot of us start to wonder if it was our fault. A lot of us feel guilty."

I explain again how I wasn't supposed to be talking to him, and the worm swells. The guidance counselor reminds me that in Pakistan sticking to the rules might be simple, but that living here in Brooklyn, seeing other ways of life, seeing other people choose different options, makes rule keeping difficult.

"From what you've said," she reminds me, "he was your friend. Truly your friend. Nothing else happened between the two of you." She means that nothing improper happened. Nothing sexual. But that doesn't matter.

"Rules are rules," I say. The worm and the bees, the fear and the shame, are making it hard for me to breathe.

She stares for a long time at a tiny stuffed caterpillar I've draped over my fingers. I hear the lunch bell ring. I hear the halls rush with kids. She's still staring at the caterpillar.

"What?" I finally ask.

"Maybe his death had absolutely nothing to do with you," she says. She touches my hand. "And maybe you will never understand why he did it."

She thinks he was crazy.

"Well, he wasn't crazy."

"What do you mean?"

"He wasn't. That's all. He was just tired. I shouldn't have talked to him. I shouldn't be here talking to you."

Somebody knocks on the office door. Another kid. A group of kids. I can hear them arguing.

"If you hadn't ever talked to him," she asks, "if you hadn't ever hidden in that closet with him, would anything be different now?"

That's when I understand what happened. As clearly as bright chalked letters on a new blackboard. Because the answer is yes. It is my fault. It is absolutely my fault.

"I can't see you anymore," I tell the guidance counselor. The kids knock louder.

"What?"

"I don't need to come anymore." I place the caterpillar back on her desk. I know what I have to do.

She tries to change my mind. I won't. I have to be perfect from now on. I can never do another improper thing. I can only make it up to him, wherever he is, by being the perfect daughter, one day the perfect wife. The perfect Muslim. I have to make my parents and my brothers, especially Nif, proud. I have to follow every single rule as perfectly as possible.

The guidance counselor asks again if I'm going to hurt myself. I promise that's not in my plan. She won't call my parents because she swore not to unless it seemed I might follow in Sarim's steps, and she can see that I won't do that. She's a person who keeps her promises. I'm safe. She tells me to come back anytime. She hugs me hard while I hear the other kids curse, kick at the door, and then shriek away.

I'm grateful to the guidance counselor for helping me. I wish I could keep meeting with her because even though she doesn't understand too much, she listens the way Sarim used to. But rules are rules. And I have to be absolutely perfect.

I write another letter on the bus home.

> *Dear Sarim,*
>
> *I am so sorry for what I put you through. I never should have hidden in the closet and talked to you. I understand now that you must have suffered terribly for disobeying the laws in order not to hurt my feelings. You saw that I needed a friend, and you broke our laws*

to be that friend. If I had known what a terrible situation
I put you in, I never would have said one word to you. If
I had known that you would end your life over it, I never
would have even looked at you. Please forgive me.

When I arrive in my room, Nif is sitting on my bed. Holding all of my blue-lined squares of paper. Unfolded and rumpled.

"How could you?" he asks.

I won't ever be rid of the shame.

Drew

MY FATHER BRINGS me with him to take in the Jag. He leans back on the hood to a half sit and keeps his arms crossed while he talks to the mechanic, a Spanish guy who's got day-old stubble on his upper lip and chin.

"You call me with an estimate before you do anything," my dad goes.

"Yes, sir," the Spanish guy says. He's got an accent. I try to wander away, but my father pulls me in under his armpit.

"If you can't reach me, you talk to my son here."

"Yes, sir," the Spanish guy says again, while my dad keeps me in a shoulder lock.

"If you get my wife on the phone, don't ask her anything." He laughs a little and then pushes me away with one of those man shoves to my head. "She can't make a decision to save her life."

"Papi," I hear, and a pair of legs from underneath a dented

Saab slides out. The legs are attached to a kid around my age in jeans, a greasy T-shirt, and a tool belt. He's got a rag in his hand.

"Papi," the kid says, sitting up, *"el tambor está rayado."*

"Lo atiendo en un minuto," the Spanish guy goes.

"That your boy?" my dad asks.

"Yes, sir."

"You let him work on the cars?"

"Yes, sir," the Spanish guy goes. "He very good."

"I don't want him on the Jag," my father tells him.

"He very good," the Spanish guy says again.

His son jumps to his feet and walks over to us. He doesn't look all that Spanish to me, except he's got dark skin. But that could just be a tan.

"I don't care how good you think he is," my dad says. "I don't want him near my car."

The mechanic looks at the Jag for a minute, like he's trying to figure something out, and then he turns to his son. *"Vas a trabajar con el carro,"* the mechanic says to the kid. *"Este pendejo no notará la diferencia."*

The kid looks at me and my dad, real friendly.

"No problem, sir." He doesn't have any accent at all. He's cool as anything, and extra polite, like he doesn't even get that my father is being a total jerk. "I won't touch the car."

*   *   *

Right before we left the house this morning, I found my mom unpacking books in my dad's new study and arranging them on his built-in shelves. She was moving sort of slow, the way she always does after he's been mad at her.

"Could you start flattening the boxes when you get back?" she'd asked.

Her right eye was the shiny color of a black olive, and her cheeks had four gray fingerprints opposite a thumbprint from where he had squeezed her face. I'd already seen her left eye last night. It had turned the shiny color of a green olive about five minutes after his first punch.

"Where do I put them after they're flat?" I asked her.

"On the landing. And see if you can get Dad to eat at the diner for lunch."

"Okay," I said. "Do you want us to bring you anything?"

"Maybe a grilled cheese." She was talking a little thick, like her jaw hurt.

"It looks good," I told her, even though mostly everything in the apartment was still in a box.

"Yep," she said. "Looks pretty good."

On Monday I wear the safest clothes I can think of. Jeans that are sort of baggy but not too baggy, a black T-shirt, and Air Jordans.

I go to the same classes almost every period with the same thirty kids. Most of them are white, even though the hallway seems pretty mixed.

"I hope you're smart," some girl tells me during second period. "Because you're in one of the smart classes."

"Shut up, Marcy," this freckly kid tells her. "Who're you?" he goes to me.

His name is Josh. He's okay. He's got some friend he keeps talking about in another smart class named Daniel and a girlfriend in that other class, too. His father owns an electronics store, and his mother's an office manager, whatever that means, and he's got a younger brother named Carl.

"What's your dad do?" he asks me, fourth period.

"Computer programmer," I go.

"What about your mom?"

"When's lunch?" I ask, because I'm not in the mood to explain "wedding consultant."

Lunch is at eleven fifty-three, and it lasts until twelve thirty-seven. I sit with Josh, his friend Daniel, and Josh's girlfriend, whose name is Katy. They ask a lot of questions. When they find out my parents bought a house in the Hamptons, along with our Brooklyn brownstone, they get stupid.

"So you're rich, right?" Daniel goes.

"Don't be rude," the girlfriend says. She swats his arm.

"Why aren't you at Garfield Union?" Josh goes.

That's some private school that wouldn't let me in so late in the year but already charged my dad for next September. Only I don't let Josh know that. I just shrug, like I'm not even really listening.

When the bell rings, I spot the kid from the garage heading toward Daniel's and Katy's classroom. He's not greasy at all anymore, and he's surrounded by girls. You can tell he's used to it. He doesn't act all loud and idiotic, the way most guys would. He acts the way I'd like to if girls noticed me. Kind of calm. Kind of like he's older or something.

"You're the Jag kid, right?" he says as we pass in the hallway.

"With the asshole father," I tell him.

He waits a second, looking at me the way his father looked at the Jag the other day, and then he goes, "Nice car."

I see him again in gym.

All the smart classes and one special ed class have gym at the same time. The smart kids are definitely mostly white. The special ed kids are mostly black or Spanish. Everyone in my ethics class back in Connecticut would go nuts over that. They'd talk about racism and injustice and everything. Even though there was only about one poor kid and three blacks in that whole district, and no Spanish students at all.

"Sam," this garage kid goes, nodding at me. We've landed in roll call lines next to each other. Josh and Daniel and Katy are behind us somewhere. We have to stand in a certain formation, so now the girls can't crowd around Sam, the way they did during lunch.

"Drew," I go, nodding back.

"Anybody jump you yet?" he asks.

I've never been in a fight in my life. I guess he can tell. I guess everybody can.

"Don't worry about it," he goes. "You're big. There's only a month left. They'll probably leave you alone."

He's wrong. Some kid who looks white but has dreadlocks starts with me before fifth period.

"Yo, Gap," he goes, shoving me hard. "Watch where the fuck you're going."

I wasn't anywhere near him. I look around for Josh, who was right there a second ago, but now he's acting like he doesn't know me. I try to keep moving, but Dreadlocks blocks my way.

"Yo, Gap," he goes again, getting real close in my face. "You want to fight?" He jabs me hard with the heel of his palm. It makes me stumble backward a little. I know my face is red as anything. I know I look like a total dork.

"Banana Republic," I mumble.

"Fight," someone yells. "Fight!"

"I said," he goes, jabbing me again, "you want to fight?"

"Not really," I tell him.

A bunch of kids start laughing like maniacs and going, "Ooohhh."

"You a fag?" the kid goes. "You talking like a fag. You a fag?"

"Are you?" I go.

"You calling me a fag!" he screams. If I weren't scared so shit-less, I'd laugh. He knocks me with both hands, and my books fall all over the place.

"Just leave him alone, Dean," I hear someone say. It's Josh's girlfriend, Katy. She's standing with Josh, whose freck-les look orange now for some reason.

"Shut up, bitch," Dreadlocks Dean goes.

Katy blushes and looks like a dork, too. I can tell she's scared. I guess the kids in the smart classes don't fight very much.

"Don't call her a bitch," I go.

"Yo, cunt," he goes, to Katy. "Pick up your man's books, cunt."

I'm pretty sure that's the last thing that happens before I nail him.

* * *

Seeing a fight in real life is different from seeing a fight on TV. On TV it looks cool. Everything happens in an order you can follow. Everything looks smooth, even for the guy who's losing. There's a punch, and then a kick, and then a headlock, and then maybe another punch. There's thuds and shouts that match what you see. Even when things get gory, even when somebody's nose starts to gush or someone's getting drowned in a toilet bowl, it all sort of looks organized. Set, in a way. Like a dance.

But in real life there's no rhythm. In real life nobody's graceful. Nobody's smooth. There's just clumsiness and mostly quiet. Nobody makes much noise at all. People slip and miss their punch and lose their balance and look like idiots. Like those old, silent movies, with a bunch of grown adults skidding on banana peels, acting like fools.

What surprises me is that when you're in the fight, you don't see anything. Not the graceful TV kind of thing or the clumsy real-life thing. What surprises me is that when you're in the fight, you lose track of time and space, almost like you're asleep or maybe even dead, and you just feel this weird ache in your arms while you use them to bash the other guy's head on the ground, and then this relief when someone finally makes you stop and you can rest again.

*   *   *

"Your mother says she's sick," the principal's secretary tells me. I've got an ice pack on my eye. I don't remember when Dreadlocks Dean punched it, but it's killing me now, so I guess he got a good one in. "She says she's sending your father."

"Will Dean be okay?" I ask.

"Paramedics said it was probably a mild concussion."

When I saw the ambulance, I freaked out. I thought I'd killed him.

"I'm really sorry," I say, even though I didn't do anything to her. "I've never been in a fight before."

"That's a laugh," she goes.

"I swear."

My father stays quiet until I'm getting out of the Range Rover, in front of our house. The goofy-faced neighbor kid stares at us from his stoop.

"So what happened?" my dad finally asks.

"Some kid called you an asshole," I tell him, slamming the door.

"Seems like you could have gotten out of that one," he yells through the window, but I can tell from his smirk that he's psyched. A UPS truck behind him starts to honk, and he honks back and then drives away.

The neighbor kid stares at me while I jiggle our lock.

He's passing a basketball fast around his middle, hands making little slapping noises each time they hit.

"Hi." He smiles. He's always smiling.

"Hi, Gingerbread," I say.

"What are you doing home?" *Slap, slap, slap.*

"I kind of got into a fight," I say. "What are you?"

"I'm kind of sick," he tells me. He's got that ball moving so fast it blurs in with his hands.

"You don't look sick," I say.

"Your eye is puffed up," he goes. *Slap, slap, slap.*

My mother coats a cucumber slice in baking soda and makes me hold it over my eye. Hers are matching colors now. Sort of a yellowish gray.

"Is this what you use?" I ask her.

"Don't be fresh," she says.

I wasn't trying to be.

Josh acts like he never left my ass out to dry. "That Dean kid is such a dick," he tells me. "He's in a million fights. He's always getting suspended."

"Why don't they just kick him out?"

"Then they'd have to kick out about a hundred kids. You only get kicked out if you have a weapon."

"A weapon?" I want to go back to Connecticut.

"Yeah. You know. Like a box cutter."

"You mean I could have gotten slashed?"

"How many fights have you been in?" he asks.

"None," I tell him.

"Very funny," he goes.

"I swear."

Later I take a long time in the bathroom until I'm pretty sure he and Daniel won't wait for me anymore. I jog out the boys' room door and nearly mow over Sam.

"Sorry," I say.

"Yo. You want to fight?" he goes, imitating Dreadlocks. I guess everyone knows about yesterday.

I don't answer, and we both keep walking.

"Lunch is the other way," he tells me.

"So where are you going?" I ask.

We don't say a word until we're sitting down on the back school steps.

"I'd give anything to drive your dad's car," he says after a while.

"Me, too."

We get quiet again. Sam is cool to be around, especially after Josh, who never shuts up. In Connecticut I only hung out with this one guy, Shep. I liked him because he was quiet, too. He was sort of not-too-bright quiet, where Sam seems pretty smart, but I liked Shep. He never invited me over, so I never had to bring him to my house.

"I guess you miss wherever you came from," Sam goes.

I shrug.

"I miss Pennsylvania sometimes," he says.

"You lived in Pennsylvania?" I ask.

"Live. In the summers. With my great-aunt and uncle. And my mom, if she can swing it."

"Why? Where is she the rest of the time?"

"Europe, mostly. She's an artist."

I never knew anybody whose mother was an artist. I never knew anybody who only sees his mom just sometimes either. Never, or on weekends maybe, but not just sometimes.

"How'd an artist end up with a mechanic?" I ask, before I even think about how that sounds. I know I turn red as anything again. Talk about rude.

But Sam doesn't seem fazed. "My dad was her slumming fling," he goes.

I don't know what a slumming fling is, so I stay quiet and pretend that I do. But I guess Sam figures it out.

"My mom's white," he explains. "She liked my dad a lot, but mostly she just thought he was interesting. You know. An exhibit from the other side."

"Oh," I go. I still don't really get it, so I change the subject. "Why aren't you eating?"

"Why aren't you?"

I shrug, and then we sit awhile without saying anything. Then he goes, "Where'd you learn to fight like that anyway?"

I start to shrug again, but then I stop. "I guess from my dad," I say, which, really, is the truth.

I help my mother put away the dishes that go on the highest shelves.

While she's handing me the champagne glasses, she goes, "You're taller than I am now."

It's true. Her nose is only as high as my chin. I stare at her messed-up face, and she turns away fast.

"Why do you put up with it?" I ask.

"I don't want to talk about that."

I set the champagne glasses on the counter. They're rimmed in gold, and they used to belong to her grandmother. Big deal.

"I want to talk about it," I go. The last time I did this was three years ago. I was eleven, and she slapped me.

"Stop it, Drew," she says.

"Why don't you just divorce him or something?"

"I don't want to divorce him," she tells me. "It's none of your business."

"How come you never call the cops?"

"I don't need the police," she goes, getting loud. "Just leave it alone!"

"People are going to notice it here," I tell her. "It's not like Connecticut, where you can hide out all the time. Where people pretend everything's fine all the time."

"I said stop it, Drew!"

"What are you going to do?" I ask her, mean. "Hit me?"

My dad finds me in our new family room with the TV on fuzz. "What's the matter with you?" he goes.

I feel like shit, that's what, I could tell him. *For the way I made Mom look today. For being a dick to her. For never knowing the right thing to do.*

"What time is it?" I ask him.

"Late. Shouldn't you be asleep?" He takes the remote and zaps the TV off.

I shrug. He leans in to examine my eye.

"Does it hurt?" His tie dangles near my mouth. I have this urge to bite it.

"Not really," I tell him.

"Wait here," he goes, and he disappears into the kitchen.

I hear him banging around in there, and when he comes back, his shoes and tie are off, and he's got two mugs. At first

I think he's brought me a beer, but mine is just soda. He flops down on the couch and stuffs a pillow behind his head.

"Look," he goes, "I'm sorry about your school situation."

I take a sip of my soda, which is flat. My mother likes it that way, so she always leaves the tops off the bottles.

"I wouldn't care if you just missed the last month, but they tell me that's against the law."

So's beating up your wife, I think.

"Don't worry about it," I tell him instead.

"I'm not *worried,*" he goes. Then he sighs. "Changes can be hard," he says. "We moved at a bad time. I know that. I'm *sorry.*"

I stay quiet and stare at his feet. There's a little hole in his sock under the big toe. A hair is sticking out of it.

"You know what I was thinking about today?" he asks me after a while.

"What?"

"I was thinking about that time we went camping. Just me and you. Remember the swing?"

It was Fourth of July weekend. I was about eight. We had a two-man tent and trail mix with M&M's in it. We each had a canteen and a sleeping bag. We used my mom's Skin-So-Soft oil to keep away the bugs and smelled like a couple of fifteen-year-old girls, according to my dad.

There was this lake, and a hill by the lake with a rope swing hanging from a branch higher than the roof of our house. There were about a million kids climbing up that muddy bank, waiting on line to fly off the rope. When you ran with it, the pebbly muck under your feet cut up your toes, but then you'd be sailing through the air, flying, floating, and you'd let go at the scariest, highest minute, and you'd fall about a zillion miles, and the water would suck you down in this freezing gulp, and you'd swallow a little of it from your Tarzan scream, or maybe from laughing, and it tasted like leftover Popsicle stick after the ice cream's been licked off.

My dad was the only grown-up in that line. He was the only father racing up the slope and throwing himself over the lake, letting out Tarzan calls and making huge splashes. The only adult who'd take me, and any other kids who weren't too scared, tucked under his arm like a football, for a two-at-a-time leap and drop.

His skin was slippery with lake water and sweat, and he smelled like old, clean undershirts, and he held you rough, his fingers gripping you tight enough to leave marks up and down your side by the end of the day. At the last minute, your nose squished into his chest, your ears sloshing with water and speed, glimmers of light flashing through the cracks between your head and his body, he'd lift and shove you away from him hard, so you wouldn't smash into each other on the way down, and you'd fall, screaming bloody murder and flailing to find the right way up before you hit the water.

"We had a great time, didn't we?" he goes.

"Yeah," I say.

"I was thinking, here you are about to start tenth grade, and we haven't done anything just you and me since then. Just father and son."

"Uh huh," I go.

"That's important," he tells me. "That father and son stuff."

"Uh huh," I go.

He wiggles his toes and then lifts his head up a little to get a better look at me.

"What I'm trying to say to you," he says, "is that I remember being your age like it was yesterday, and it sucked. And I didn't have anyone to talk to, and I could have *used* someone." He sits up now and takes a long swig from his mug. Then he burps. "So I just want you to know, you can come to me. I *want* you to come to me."

The reason why it was just us alone that July Fourth was that he'd beaten her up a few days before. She had bruises all over, so she couldn't go out.

I remember wanting so bad for him never to come out of

the water after a drop. Wanting him to be drowned and dead, down deep in the swampy bottom, so he'd never hit her again. And I remember feeling unbelievably guilty for being so happy when he'd pop up, spitting and whipping his wet hair out of his eyes, the coolest, best, most fun dad ever to fly me out in space higher and faster than I ever could have gone on my own.

Sam shows me around his dad's shop.

"Cálmate, Papi," he says to his father, who doesn't look so psyched to see me at first. *"El es cool. No es como su padre."*

They fix about twelve cars at once. Sam tells me his dad does a lot of it, but they have three mechanics—two Puerto Ricans and one guy from Albania who was a college math professor back home but can't find work here. Sam mostly does body repairs, not engine work. But I think he knows more than he's letting on.

"When it's fixed, let's drive it," I tell him, while we stand around the Jag. The wheels are off, and it's hiked up on one of those poles.

"Yeah, right," Sam goes.

A woman wearing skinny pink glasses and holding a briefcase steps into the garage.

"I'm serious," I say while she looks around. "We'll take it out before you tell my dad it's ready."

"I bet you don't even know how to drive," Sam says.

"Excuse me," the woman goes.

"So?" I say. "You do."

"Excuse me." The woman walks up to us. "You're Samuel?"

"Samuel?" I go, but as usual, Sam doesn't even blink.

He just shrugs at me, and then, real polite, he says to the woman, "Sam." He holds out his hand. "You must know my mom."

The woman shakes with him, smiling. "Annie," she tells him. "Your mother was supposed to have written you that I'd be coming by."

"I wrote her back to forget it," Sam says. "No offense or anything."

She's sort of staring at him through those pink frames. Something about the way she's looking makes my face get hot, but Sam is calm as anything.

"Sam," I go, but then I don't know what to say next.

"Your mother wasn't exaggerating," this Annie woman tells him. "I thought maybe she was using artistic license to serve maternal subjectivity."

I don't know what that's supposed to mean, and I can't tell if Sam gets it either because he sort of ignores it.

"I'm really not that interested," he says, but the woman's already pulling a card out of the side pocket of her briefcase.

"She made me promise to come take a look at you and to be encouraging if I thought you could work," this woman says, handing him the card.

Sam holds it out so I can see it, too. Cooke Model Management Corporation, it says. Annie Sherman, Booking Agent.

"I got the impression from your mother that you and your father could use some money."

I look over at Sam, while he looks up at her.

"There's a lot of money in modeling, you know," she tells him.

Josh and Daniel are pissed that I don't hang with them. They're extra pissed because I guess Sam used to stay by himself and have all those girls, only now, since I sit with Sam at lunch, the girls are all over me, too. I know they're not there for me, really, but it's sort of fun. I stay quiet, to make sure I don't look like a jerk and to watch how Sam handles things. Mostly he's pretty cool to everybody. He never joins in with one girl trashing another. He never treats one better than the other. I wonder if he'll let it slip that he's going to try to be a model. That he has some interview coming up at his mother's friend's agency. I bet girls love that kind of thing. But Sam keeps his mouth shut. I guess he has all the attention he needs from them.

"What do you think of that redhead with the contact

lenses?" I ask him one day, near the last week of school. We're walking to his dad's shop.

"She's okay," he goes.

I think she's hot. I'd ask her out, only I'm too shy, and I don't want a girlfriend anyway, because if she bugged me, I'm worried about what I'd do. So I just jerk off thinking about her instead. It always starts off with me asking what color her eyes really are, and then she takes out her contact lenses, and then she goes, *As long as I'm taking things off* . . . and she steps out of her jeans, and then . . .

"She's totally into you," I say. "I bet she'd go all the way with you."

"All the way?" he says. He's always making fun of how I talk. "That means 'fuck,' right?"

"Shut up," I tell him.

"Okay, for real. Forget her. There's someone else I like," he says.

"Who?"

"This Indian girl. She sits at that corner table during lunch."

"One of those veil girls?"

"She doesn't wear a veil."

"You know what I mean."

"Her name is Sonia."

"That eighth grader?"

"Yeah."

"How do you even know her?"

"We had some art elective together once. She's smart. Real smart. She's fine, too," he tells me. "You ever get a really good look at her?"

"Those girls don't go out with people," I remind him.

"Yeah," he says, like he figured it out a long time ago. "I know."

We turn the corner into the shop, and Sam's dad knocks on Sam's head with his knuckles. *"Nos llegaron dos nuevas,"* he goes. *"Todo carrocería. ¿Los quieres?"*

"He's got some new cars in," Sam tells me. "All body work. You want to help out or something?"

His dad unfists his hand from that knuckle rap and puts his palm flat on top of Sam's head and just keeps it there. They're both raising their eyebrows at me, and for the first time they kind of look alike.

Suddenly I can see them knocking on our door to tell us the Jag is ready. I can see my mom opening the door, thinking it's my dad who forgot his key. They stare at her banged-up face and get a good look before she ducks away.

Your car's ready, Sam would say to me.

Very good car, his dad would say.

Thanks, I'd go, trying to close the door fast.

Was that your mom? Sam would ask.

Yeah, I'd say, wondering how to get them out of there.

Who did that to her?

Nobody, I'd tell them.

His father would say something to Sam in Spanish. Then his father would put his hand flat on top of my head. It would feel heavy and warm.

You call us if it happens again, Sam would say. *Or call the police.*

What are you talking about? I'd go. *She just hit the dashboard when my father crashed the Jag.*

You should call the police, Sam would say.

It's not that simple, I'd tell him, thinking about my father in jail and both my parents hating me forever.

"Drew?" Sam's going. "You want to hang out?"

"Nah," I lie. "I've got to go."

We spend most of Memorial Day weekend unpacking the Hamptons house and buying it new furniture. My mother's face is back to normal, and my parents are in a good mood. On Saturday afternoon my father sneaks me away with him to toss the football around on the beach while my mom conference calls with some new wedding clients about flower arrangements. Walking close to the surf, my dad pulls me in under his arm and asks me to start thinking about what I want for my fifteenth birthday. "I want you to stop hitting her," I tell him, but the wind by the ocean and the breakers are pretty loud, and I don't think he hears.

After soft-shell crab in a restaurant with a sunset and ocean view, they hold hands while we walk through the town center past ice-cream shops and antiques stores. I walk a little ahead of them so nobody knows they belong to me.

"You're not *embarrassed,* are you?" my mom calls out.

"Stop it, Mom," I say, trying to be loud enough so she can hear, but not so loud the whole street can.

They speed up and skip next to me, swinging their arms, just to embarrass me more.

"Come on," I tell them.

People are looking at us now. My father kisses my mother right there in middle of the street.

"I'm walking back," I warn them.

They laugh.

In about three weeks, she'll answer the phone wrong, or buy the wrong kind of toothpaste, or bring the wrong shirt to the wrong dry cleaners, and he'll bash her all over again.

In the back of the Range Rover, on the way home to Brooklyn, I try to figure out what to do. That's how I usually spend my time in a car lately, thinking about what to do. Maybe that's because the first time I saw him hit her was while we were all driving somewhere.

I was little. Four, or maybe five. We were going to Vermont for my first ski trip. My father had asked my mother to drive for a while, and then he got mad at her because she didn't put on her turn signal. Then he got mad because she changed the radio station, and then, after she didn't have the right change for the toll, he got mad again. When she said it was impossible to drive safely with him yelling at her like that, he fist-hit her smack in the jaw, and she swerved, and my stomach felt like it was on a sideways elevator, and he told her she better learn to drive safely no matter what he did, and he hit her again, and she swerved again, and I thought and thought about what to do, and by the time we reached the ski lodge, I still hadn't figured it out, and when my father told everybody we'd had a little accident and that she'd hit the dashboard, and my mother let him keep the lie, I started to cry, and someone at the ski lodge gave me a Tootsie Pop, and I still didn't know what to do.

Sam's going to his aunt and uncle's tomorrow in Pennsylvania, but the Jag is finished this morning.

Over the phone he'd wanted me to tell my father it was ready, but I didn't. I just walked to the shop on my own, like it was a regular day. Only it doesn't feel like a regular day. I don't feel regular. I feel mad. I was mad the minute I heard Sam's voice on the phone. I don't know why exactly, but I'm sick of his voice. I'm sick of him.

"You ready to drive it?" I ask Sam at the garage.

"You're killing me," he goes.

"Just drive it," I say. "You know you want to."

"Nah." He shakes his head. "It'll get you into trouble."

"I don't care."

"I do," he goes.

"What's your problem?" I ask him.

"Huh?"

"You have to do the right thing every time?" I sound like an asshole. I can't help it.

"What are you talking about?" he goes.

"You have to be so perfect?"

His father slides out from underneath some car on the other side of the garage. *"¿Tienes algún problema?"* he yells over to Sam.

"No es nada, Papi," Sam yells back.

"Do you ever break one goddamn rule?" I'm going. "Do you ever just do something for the fun of it?"

He gets real still.

"My whole life is a goddamn broken rule," he tells me, real low, real calm. Then he steps in close, like Dreadlocks Dean did that day, and his voice stays quiet, but it's hard and mad as anything. "Do you know how *fun* it is to be a bastard half spic with a mother who'd rather fingerpaint in some other country than live near you and a father who has to kiss rich white ass daily just so he can make his goddamn rent?" He backs up, glaring at me with this disgusted look, like he's the coach and I'm the spaz retard.

"You always know what to say, don't you?" I tell him, sarcastic as hell. "I'd take it all. I'd take his life any day. I'd take his father in a second. "You always know what to do." I want to be him so bad it makes my blood hurt. "With the girls, with the cars, with me. With everyone."

He sort of blinks, and then he shakes his head, like he's sorry for me or something. "Whatever," he goes, and then suddenly I get scared I'll either start bawling or else rip his face off.

"You know what?" I tell him. "From now on just stay the fuck away." And I'm gone.

I'm so pissed off I don't even get what's going on until I'm in the apartment and the door is closed. My parents are in the foyer, and he's mad again. She's got blood on her mouth and over her eye, and her sleeve is torn. She's got the keys and mail table between them, holding it up by the surface so the legs stick out to sort of protect her, but he's twisting it out of her grip.

"Go to your room," she tells me, the way she always does.

He yanks the table away from her and tosses it behind him. Then he grabs her and shoves her up against the wall. She throws up her hands, and I walk around them into the kitchen. I hear the punch, which doesn't sound like much in real life but turns eyes the shiny color of olives in five minutes flat, and I pick up the phone.

I dial that stupid, stupid number they make TV shows off of and try to keep my voice steady, so if they replay it on the news, I won't sound like an idiot.

"What is the location of the emergency?" they go, without saying hello.

"Two-fifty-one Baker Place," I say. "Between Seventh and Eighth Avenue."

"What's the nature of the emergency?" they ask.

"My dad's beating the shit out of my mother," I go.

"Stay on the line, please," they tell me.

So I do.

My mother starts to cry when they cuff him. She never cries.

That goofy Gingerbread kid watches from his stoop. He's got his basketball tucked under one arm, and I can see his fingers tapping it, fast, like he's typing or sending Morse code.

My father stops in front of me as they walk him to the squad car. They let him lean down to whisper in my ear. The kid stops tapping and shifts the ball to his other arm.

"Do you see what you've done?" my dad goes, really quiet, nodding over to her. She's still crying, slumped against our front door. "Do you see?"

Year Three

Grace

China

Ebony

Sam

Carl

Monique

Molly

Drew

Caitlin

Hector

Grace

MY MOTHER IS a lunatic. She has a routine for everything, and if you do anything to screw it up, she falls apart. My mom falling apart is something you don't want to see. The problem is, her routine's always changing, so it's next to impossible to figure out what you might be doing to screw it up. Which means you never know when she's going to fall apart.

She's a receptionist at some fancy ad agency on Madison Avenue in the city. I'm sure her stupid routines must get screwed up at work, but Madison Avenue probably doesn't let her get away with any falling apart. They should use her in one of their ads. For a psych ward.

She'll come home one day and fall apart because I didn't make dinner for us. Then the next day she'll fall apart because I made dinner but she was planning on ordering in pizza.

Then the next day she'll fall apart because she called ahead of
time to tell me to order pizza, but I ordered it from the wrong
place. I'm not allowed to defend myself. When I try, she says,
"Don't talk back! I don't want to hear it!" Then she stomps
down the hall to Walker's apartment.

I don't know how he can stand her, but he's kept her for
over two years. He works for the city or something. He's okay,
but he takes up too much of my mom's time. Even though
she's a lunatic, I never really get to see her, and that sort of
bothers me. I keep thinking if we had more time, I could talk
to her about certain things that Ebony and China talk about
to their mothers.

One thing I'd want to tell her about is how it can be at school.
I know we can't afford private school or anything, but the girls
here are really hard on me. Somebody's always wanting to fight.
Somebody's always calling me stuck up or a bitch. It's bad enough
I'm white, but I think the way I look makes it worse. When I
used to go with my mother to the city sometimes, people would
stop me on the street. They would give my mother their cards.
They always wanted to know what agency I was with.

It's nice being good-looking because it's one less thing
to worry about. But it's hard, too, because when you stand
out in ninth grade, people always want to start with you. If
you're a cute guy, it doesn't matter how you act. But if you're

a pretty girl, things are different. If you're too nice, they call you weak. If you're not nice enough, they say you think you're better than they are. The whole thing sucks. The only way out of it is to get famous. If I started getting modeling jobs and got famous, then I'd be a celebrity instead of just a pretty white girl, and then they'd want me to be their friend instead of wanting to start with me. So I got accepted with this fancy agency a couple of weeks ago, and I'm waiting for them to get me work. My mother is excited because she thinks I could make enough money to send myself to college. Walker doesn't like it. "Keep your head on straight," he keeps telling me. He thinks I'm going to make it.

Ebony and China are the best. They understand me pretty well, and they never give me a hard time. I told them right off the bat, way back in sixth grade, that my mom might be weird around them. I figure it's better to let people know up front and let them decide if they want to have anything to do with you. I told them how my mother's a fake. How she'll say all the right things but she's kind of racist. How they'd see through her in a second. I was nervous maybe they'd dump me after that, but they were cool. By ninth grade there's not that many groups that are mixed. Everybody usually ends up with their own. Me and Ebony and China are one of three mixed groups left. We don't care.

We spend the most time at Ebony's house. She's got eight-year-old twin sisters, and her mother's a real estate agent. Ebony's mother is really cool. She knows a lot of poetry from when she used to be a teacher, and she uses it on Ebony when she's trying to make a point. Ms. Giles keeps the twins' artwork stuck to the refrigerator with magnets that look like orange slices dipped in chocolate. Ms. Giles's first name is Grace, just like me.

China's mother is nice but not as cool as Ebony's. She's a pharmacist. She brings home all kinds of sample medicine all the time, and when China is sick, they never have to get prescriptions. China's mother has really short hair, and she wears big earrings. She calls China baby, and she called Ebony that once, too, when Ebony was crying because her dad had called the night before, drunk, from somewhere in North Carolina. I never had a father. Just some man who slept with my mother once, and she didn't know she was pregnant until he was long gone anyway. China's father is a cameraman for *Sunset.* I've only seen him a couple of times. He's got a pierced ear, and he has the same slanty eyes as China, and he calls China's mother baby.

When China screws up, she gets grounded and loses her allowance. China gets ten dollars a week. Ebony gets seven. I don't get an allowance. I have to ask when I need money for something. Depending on whether my mother's routine got messed up, I either get it or I don't.

My mom is partly crazy because she's an alcoholic. She's not drinking now because she went through all these programs that the ad agency had to pay for. She's been sober for five years. But once you're an alcoholic, you're always an alcoholic. She still has to go to AA meetings once a week and twice on holidays. That's another reason why she's so busy. She's got work, AA meetings, and her therapy, too. She's been in therapy for five years. I went with her once. Her therapist was this woman who had a birthmark on the left side of her lip, spreading into her cheek. I didn't hear a word she said because I was busy trying to figure out if that birthmark was getting bigger right in front of my eyes or if I was just imagining it. I squinted a lot, trying to see it from all angles, and my mother said later the woman thought I had a twitch. My mother was laughing so hard when she told me that, she wet her pants. She showed me the stain.

I remember the last time my mother was drunk. I was eight, and we were at the Bronx Zoo. My mother was walking too fast for me. She wouldn't stop to see the animals. I wanted to look at the elephants and the gorillas. I wanted to just watch them for a little while. But my mother wouldn't stop. She made us walk and walk and walk. I needed to use the bathroom, but she wouldn't let me. After a while I could barely lift my feet. They were scuffing the ground when a man told my mother it looked like her pretty little girl was tired. *Keep your goddamn hands off her!* my mother screamed at him. Then she threw up. Then she fell asleep. It was right in front of the elephants, so I got to look at them for a while before they came to get us.

China says me and Ebony have a lot of anger. China reads college books, and she always knows stuff about people and life and that kind of thing, the way your grandmother might know. I guess China is wise, more than smart, but she's pretty smart, too.

We always meet under the bleachers during lunch because it's private, plus we see all kinds of good stuff from under there, like Mr. Stappio feeling up Ms. Manning and Denny Stephens selling coke to Mercedes Little.

Today me and China take our hot dogs into the gym and stoop over to Ebony, who's concentrating really hard on pulling a razor blade across her wrist. I just stand here like an idiot, not even believing what I'm seeing, while China smacks Ebony's hand, and the blade flies and then skids out from under the bleachers.

"Bitch," Ebony complains, like cutting herself is no big

deal. "I wasn't done." Two thin lines bead red onto her skin, like a liquid bracelet.

"Are you trying to kill yourself?" China hisses. "Because if you're trying to kill yourself, you better tell us now. Right now!"

I clamp one of my cafeteria napkins over Ebony's wrist.

"Damn," China says, while I pat down on top of the cuts. There isn't much seeping through, just enough to make the napkin stick.

"Bitch," Ebony grumbles again. "I'm not trying to kill myself."

I start breathing again. I didn't know I'd stopped.

"Doesn't it hurt?" I ask. I'm the weakest out of the three of us.

"It hurts"—Ebony sniffs, all proud—"but it feels nice, too. Like when you get tickled until you could die."

"You're crazy," I tell her. "Apologize."

"Sorry," Ebony says.

"Tell us you're not going to do it again," I order.

"It feels nice," Ebony argues. "Especially when you're mad."

"Tell us!" I say.

"I won't do it again."

"You better not," China goes.

"What are you mad at anyway?" I ask.

Ebony shrugs.

"Her asshole father," China says. "Right?"

"I don't know."

"Bet you he called again last night, right?"

Another shrug.

"Was he drunk?"

He was probably whining about all the letters he supposedly sends that Ebony never gets. We spent practically all of seventh grade hating Ebony's mother, thinking she was throwing those letters away, before we figured out Ebony's father never wrote a mad scrap.

"Both of y'all," China says, "ought to get into therapy."

She's said that before. She thinks you can't have an alcoholic parent and not need therapy. I used to wonder who she thought is more screwed up, me or Ebony. But now with this razor blade thing, it's pretty obvious.

Ebony grabs my cheese puffs bag and pulls it apart while I shift my weight a little. The bleachers are hard and sharp in your back or your side. You have to move around a lot underneath them if you want to stay comfortable. I start to snatch the cheese puffs back, but Ebony's fingertips, already dusted orange, change my mind. They're bitten so bloody it makes you hurt all over, just looking at them.

"You shouldn't be cutting yourself," I say. "It's fucked up. You don't have to get all fucked up."

China says something better. "If I ever see you do that again," she warns Ebony, "I'm telling your mother."

There are two messages on the answering machine when I get home from school. I eat a chocolate chip granola bar and listen to them, careful to keep my crumbs over the wastebasket. The first message is from my mom, telling me not to make crumbs when I get home from school. The next message is from my agency, telling me to be at some building in Manhattan the next day at three-thirty, and to be sure to wear my hair down, a white shirt, and no makeup. I never wear makeup.

I'm on the phone in my room when my mother gets home from work. I'm talking to China.

"Why a white shirt?" I'm asking.

"I don't know. Maybe it's for some sort of laundry ad or something."

"Grace!" my mom yells from the kitchen. I can hear the answering machine beeping its finishing beeps.

"Why's she mad this time?" China asks.

"Same reason as always," I tell her. "No reason." We laugh.

"Damn it, Grace!"

China and I hang up, and in two seconds my mother is

standing in my doorway. She looks like me, only she's not pretty. I never could figure that out.

"Why didn't you call me at work to tell me about your audition?"

"I didn't know I was supposed to."

"I told you to call me immediately if you got something."

She never said that. I don't answer back because if you stay quiet, you have a better chance of her staying calm. She sighs some dramatic sigh and storms out of my room. I walk into the hallway and begin to count to myself, in Mississippis. Usually I don't get up to twenty before she's yelling about something else. Boom. On eleven she starts up from her room.

"It's six," she complains. "It's Wednesday!"

"You said six-thirty last week," I answer from my spot in the hall. I've stood there so much there's a worn patch on the wood floor under my feet.

"Six o'clock!" She stomps into view. "Why do you always have to make everything so hard for me? Damn it. You do this on purpose."

I walk slow down the hall from our apartment to Walker's, wondering why the neighbors don't complain about me and my mom. I know they hear her. They used to hear me, but I stopped yelling back a while ago. Walker's as bad as the neighbors. He acts like he doesn't know anything either, but I bet he does.

"Time for dinner," I tell him when he opens his door. He's tall and skinny and has a goatee.

"I thought we decided six-thirty."

"Talk to her," I answer.

He's quiet for a minute, looking at me.

"What?"

"Nothing."

"She just got home," I explain. "Nothing's even ready yet."

"We'll order pizza."

Later, through all of my mom's bitching about how she's going to have to miss work to take me to my call, Walker congratulates me.

"Well, I didn't get anything yet," I go.

"You got a call," my mom says. "And I'm sure you'll get the job, whatever it is. Walker's absolutely right. Congratulations."

"If I get it," I hear myself asking, "can I invite Ebony and China over to celebrate?"

"Another slice?" my mother offers Walker.

He looks over at me. "What about it, Judy?" he asks my mom. "Can she?"

"No more?" My mom picks up the last slice with the tips of her fingers. "I'll eat it then."

Walker and I clean up the kitchen while she takes her shower.

"She's racist," I tell Walker, handing him a dish towel and a wet plate.

"I wouldn't say that," Walker answers.

"She is. That's why she doesn't like them."

"I don't think your mom's racist."

"Why does she hate my friends then?"

Walker concentrates on drying. He makes the plate squeak, he rubs so hard.

"She acted like she didn't even hear me."

"She has a lot on her mind," he says.

A plate slips from my fingers, and for a second Walker and I freeze. There's no telling how long my mom will go off if it breaks. But it just clatters in those edge-to-edge circles on the floor until I manage to grab it into silence. We hold still for a while, listening to see if she heard anything from the shower. Nothing.

"How can you stand her?" I ask him.

For a minute I think he might slap me. Instead he puts his hands on my shoulders. "I love her," he says. "And so do you."

The next day I bring a note to my homeroom teacher excusing me from school after fourth period. When the bell rings, me and China and Ebony sneak out the fire doors to Ebony's house for lunch. Her mom is cool with us leaving school grounds to eat sandwiches instead of cafeteria food. She's finishing her coffee when we walk in.

"Congratulations, Grace!" She smiles.

"It's just a call," I say. "I don't have the job yet or anything."

"Y'all hungry?" she asks, putting her coffee mug into the sink and grabbing plates and glasses to put around the table. Me and Ebony and China start pulling bologna and tomatoes and stuff out of the refrigerator.

"If I get it," I say before I can stop myself, "my mom's going to take us all out to celebrate." Nobody misses a beat.

"Cool," China goes.

"I'm ordering steak," Ebony goes.

Ms. Giles unscrews a mayonnaise jar and says, "'Hope, caught under the jar's rim, crawls like a golden fly.'"

"Mom!" Ebony moans, reaching up into the freezer to grab some ice.

"What does she mean?" I ask.

"Dream on," China translates for me, and then Ebony's mom grabs Ebony's wrist.

"What is this?"

"Nothing," Ebony says, pulling away.

Her mother glares at me and China. "What is that?"

China shrugs, while I blush. Sometimes I hate being white.

"Cat scratch," Ebony says, smooth as a pearl.

"Then why is Grace's face so red?"

"I'm hot," I say quickly. I try to catch a glimpse of that wrist to make sure it still has only two scratches. Ebony's covering it up with her palm.

"You. Children. Are not starting that tattoo nonsense in this house," Ms. Giles says, pointing three fingers hard at all of us. "Do you understand me!"

Then she glances over at the kitchen clock and grabs her coat.

"I mean it," she warns, smacking Ebony's head lightly with her palm on the way out.

A few minutes after she leaves, when Ebony's taking a chomp out of her sandwich, I see four more scratches. Fine and thin, like dark hairs. I kick China, who glances over to check things out for herself. Ebony notices us looking and shakes her head at China.

"Don't you dare tell her," she says.

"You promised," China accuses.

"You going to be a bitch?" Ebony asks.

"She's being a friend, bitch," I snap.

"Both of y'all can leave then," Ebony says. She says it quiet.

"I'm not going anywhere," China goes.

"My call isn't until three-thirty," I remind Ebony.

"Leave," Ebony orders us.

We sit there through every last crumb, and nobody remembers to wish me luck when it's time to go.

In the waiting area my mother puts on a good show. She keeps her arm around my shoulders and plays with my hair. She wants people to think we're really close.

"It's our first call," she gushes to the receptionist. I want to kill her.

There are about three million other girls there, all in white shirts except a few, who look completely embarrassed. One of them is slinking out the door when my mother and I get there. They all have long brown hair and are really pretty. A lot of them wear makeup. A lot of them are alone and look bored. One of them has a miniature television set. She's watching *Sally Jessy Raphael.* She has the volume up pretty loud. All of them stare at me when I walk in.

"I was just wondering what the product is," my mother says to the receptionist.

The receptionist shrugs. "Got me."

"You'd think they'd let us know what the product is," my mother says, looking around at some of the other mothers for support. Nobody bothers.

We wait and wait and wait. Sometimes a girl disappears down this long hallway and is gone for fifteen minutes. Other times a girl is back practically before she even left. By the time they call my name, there are only three or four of us left.

My mother walks fast. I have to work hard to keep up with her. The audition room isn't any big deal. It has wide windows and a wooden desk, and there are five people sitting in folding chairs along the wall. A man with a goatee like Walker's takes one look at me, stands up, and says, "She's the one."

It's just like in the movies. I can't believe it. The others are nodding.

"What's the product?" my mother asks.

"Don't you need me to walk or turn or anything?" I say. I know I should probably be quiet, but it doesn't seem right. They're just handing this to me. They aren't asking me to do anything, even.

"What's the product?" my mother asks again.

"Perfume," the man with the goatee says. "For teens. It's called Future."

"I don't really wear perfume," I tell them.

They laugh like it's the funniest thing in the world. My mother tries hard not to glare at me.

"She's definitely the one," the goatee man says, looking over at the others. "Right?" They all nod.

"Usually we let you know through the agency," the goatee man tells my mother. "We'll make it official tomorrow morning." Then he turns to me. "But you're the one."

Before we leave, I find out that the people sitting down are the client, the producer, the client's lawyer, and the artistic designer. The director is the goatee man. It's a TV commercial, not a magazine ad. Which means more money and, if I don't screw up, more work, too.

"Why did I have to wear a white shirt?" I ask the director.

"You didn't," the director says. "Our people made a mistake."

I can't help it. I roll my eyes. The director rolls his right back, which makes me smile. He looks like I just shot him or something.

"You have a stunning mouth," he says, "but don't smile on the shoot."

"Rude," my mother accuses as soon as we get home. Walker's there, with sparkling cider as a stand-in for champagne, since my mom isn't allowed to even have one sip of anything alcoholic.

"I got it," I tell him.

"I knew you would," he says.

"You could have lost the whole thing, telling them you don't wear perfume."

"It just came out, Mom."

"And you gave him that *face!*"

"He didn't mind."

"How do you think that makes me look?"

"I made a great dinner," Walker interrupts. "I thought we could celebrate."

"It doesn't matter," I try. "They gave it to me, didn't they?"

"Don't tell me it doesn't matter," my mother snaps. "Don't tell me what matters!" Her voice is getting witchy.

"Judy," Walker says, using his let's-just-stay-calm tone. Sometimes, coming from him, it works.

"Don't Judy me," she spits at him.

"I got the job," I remind her. And then I can't help myself. "Nobody was thinking about you. They were thinking about me."

"That's it," she says, and her voice goes really soft. When her voice gets soft instead of louder, it's way worse. I can feel myself stiffen up, even though she hasn't hit me for a long time. "Forget it."

There's this big silence. Walker and I look at each other.

"Forget what?" I finally ask.

"Forget the job," she says. "You're not doing it."

"What?"

"You're not doing it."

"What about college money?"

"It doesn't matter," she singsongs, making fun of me.

"Judy, that hardly seems fair," Walker tries.

"Don't you start with me!" she yells at him.

I don't yell. I can't. I can hardly get the words out.

"You're a goddamn bitch," I whisper. "And I hate you."

She hits me hard. With her fist. The force of it knocks me off my feet, and I stumble backward onto the floor. The part of my head above my left ear feels like it's been blown up. I don't cry. I just stare at her until she walks into her room. Walker helps me stand, and then he leaves.

I hide out under the bleachers the next morning waiting for China and Ebony to find me. They show up for second period.

"You didn't get it?" China says.

"I got it."

"Why are you skipping?"

We don't usually cry in front of each other. I'm trying hard not to start.

"What happened?" Ebony asks. They both look pretty worried.

"My mother's a fucking bitch."

"You want us to stay?"

"Will you trade off?" I ask. "It's safer that way."

China stays first.

"Do it anyway," she tells me. "Screw your mom."

"I should call child welfare," I say. "They could let me live with Walker while she's in jail."

"Bad idea," China says. "They'd probably put you in some other home, and you'd get abused or something."

"She hates me." I never said that out loud before.

"She does not," China says, but I nod my head.

"When I was little. When she was still drinking." I stop talking because maybe it's just too stupid to say.

"What?" China goes.

She used to cuddle me, and then all of a sudden she would shove me off her lap and start screaming.

"What?" China goes again.

"She used to call me a bitch and a slut and piece of shit and a pain in the ass not worth having," I whisper. My head hurts.

China puts her hand on my palm. Her fingernails are baby blue with miniature clouds airbrushed on the tips. She saved three weeks of allowance for that sky.

"She talked shit to you?" China breathes.

I nod.

"Baby." China kisses my cheek. "You should have told me before."

"Sorry," I say.

She smacks my leg. Lightly. "Shut up."

*　*　*

Ebony slides in for the next shift, holding a candy bar.

"I'm not hungry," I tell her.

"Carl likes you," she says, peeling the wrapper down, like it's a banana.

"Everybody likes me," I moan.

"Poor you, bitch," she says.

"Did China tell you everything?"

She takes a bite of the chocolate. "Yeah. You should have told us before."

"You guys think this shit doesn't happen to white people."

"White people have no faith in their friends."

I notice fresh scratches on her wrist. The wrapper of the candy bar is brushing up against them. Ebony sees me looking.

"If you tell China, you won't need your mother to kill you," she tells me.

"Show me," I say.

"Huh?"

"Show me how to do it."

Ebony finishes chewing before she answers.

"It hurts, girl," she reminds me. "You wouldn't like it."

"Don't be a bitch," I tell her.

She makes a big show out of rolling her eyes and sucking her teeth, but when I won't take it back, she pulls a teeny tiny cardboard box from her butt pocket. The blades are each wrapped in smaller strips of cardboard and stacked up tight next to each other. She slides one out of the pack and hands it to me.

"Hold it careful, so it doesn't cut your fingers," she says, pointing to the dull sides. "Don't press too deep. Just press hard enough that it hurts, but not so hard you get yourself bleeding so you can't stop. Then there's a mess."

I decide to do it on my ankle, where socks will cover things up better than sleeves. My fingers shake a little on the first cut. I don't want them to because I don't want Ebony making fun of me. She pretends not to notice, though, and finishes up her candy bar on my second cut, which is straighter and more even. Even though it hurts, Ebony's right about the pain. It hurts, but the hurt is good, too. I stop after I have three red threads, feeling way better.

"It makes my mouth taste like metal," I tell Ebony.

She scrunches up her face. "You're crazy," she says, and then the bell rings.

At home there's a message on the machine, telling my mother the time, date, and place of my shoot: two weeks away in the city. I stare at the answering machine for a long time. I play the tape again. Then I dial the phone.

"This is Grace Sanborn," I tell the secretary at my agency. "I got a call about the Future commercial."

"Oh, yes, Grace. Congratulations."

"Did this get okayed by my mom?"

The secretary laughs, the same laugh I've heard teachers use with me after parent-teacher night.

"Absolutely," the secretary says. "We've been talking with her all day."

China sees my ankle while we're getting dressed after gym. She slams me up against a locker.

"What the fuck is that?" she whispers, pinning me against the metal. The round lock digs into my back. Some of the other kids start to gather around. People love a fight.

"Get off me," I say. "Everybody's looking."

"We're supposed to go to college," she hisses.

"Come on," I say, wriggling a little to shake her off. It doesn't work.

"Fight," some eighth graders begin to chant. "Fight. Fight. Fight."

That lock is killing me.

"You can't go to college if you're all fucked up," she breathes, mean, into my ear.

"Plenty of fucked-up people go to college," I tell her. Her

breath smells like mint gum. "My mother went to college."

She slams me again, and my head smacks backward.

"Bitch," she tells me, and then she's crying.

Ms. Evans and Ms. Lumus pull us apart and break up the crowd. China won't stop crying, and I can't start.

"I'm sorry," I keep telling her. "I'm sorry. I'm sorry. I'm sorry."

In my imagination I tell my mother everything.

I had a fight, sort of, with China today.

You did? What about?

It's kind of hard to say.

Try anyway.

You might get upset.

I won't this time. I promise.

She was pissed at me because I did something weird and bad.

What did you do?

I don't want to tell you that part yet.

Okay. Why did you do it?

Because you make me so mad all the time. And you never listen to me. You don't like me.

Oh, honey. I'm so sorry. I do like you. I love you. I'll try harder. I really will.

I'm scared to tell you the other part.

Which part?
The thing that I did.
Just try.
Okay. I cut myself.
What do you mean, you cut yourself?
I made scratches in my ankle on purpose with a razor blade.
Why?
I don't know.
I'm not really sure what happens after that.

On the morning of the shoot, our bell rings while my mother's in the bathroom. Our buzzer doesn't work, so I have to run down the two sets of stairs.

"What are you guys doing here?" I ask.

"We wanted to wish you good luck," China says. We've had a weird truce since the fight. We talk and don't talk at the same time. Ebony's been filling in the gaps, jabbering a mile a minute and calling us all kinds of bitches. She's still cutting herself, and China hasn't told on her yet. I haven't cut myself again, but I've sat with Ebony a few times to watch her. It always makes my mouth water.

"When you get famous, you better remember us little people," Ebony tells me.

"I wish you guys could come with me," I answer, meaning it.

"Grace!" We hear my mother shriek from two flights up.

"No, thanks," China says, and we crack up.

My mom and I are trapped in a cramped room for hours before anyone comes to get me. I don't have a book or a magazine or anything. Neither does my mother. There's a makeup mirror lining one wall. It has small bulbs framing it, all the way around. My mom and I keep looking at each other's reflection in that mirror.

"Want to play a word game?" she asks.

I shrug. We haven't said much to each other since she hit me.

"How about I Spy?" she suggests.

What a stupid idea. There isn't anything to spy in here anyway.

"Okay," my mom begins, as if I've agreed. "I spy something round."

"The fire alarm on the ceiling," I guess.

She frowns into the mirror at me.

Someone knocks on the door and then opens it right away, without waiting for an answer. He looks about fifteen, and he is *fine*.

"Ooops," he says. "Sorry. I thought this one was mine." He has skin the color of our wood stairs, and his hair is kind of messy, and he has big green eyes. I can't wait to tell China and Ebony.

"I'm Sam," he tells us. "I'm the other talent." That's what they call actors and models on shoots: "The talent."

"I'm Grace," I say. "That's my mother."

She blushes when he shakes her hand, and I want to die.

They make us wait a lot all morning, and while we're waiting, Sam and I figure out that we go to the same school. We've never seen each other, though, because he's a grade ahead of me and is in all the smart classes, so we've never had the same elective. Even though we both have second lunch, I always eat under the bleachers, and he's always in the lunchroom or on the back stairs by the gym. I know our school is pretty big— it's eighth through twelfth grade—but still, it's hard to believe me and Ebony and China never noticed this guy.

"How can we not have seen each other around?" I ask him.

He shrugs this sexy shrug and smiles. His smile is amazing.

But it turns out that he isn't allowed to use it. Neither of us is. We're just supposed to hang out in all these different poses with each other and look bored. That's what the director says. I never took an acting class in my life, and I'm not too sure how to look bored, but the director tells me not think about it. Just to feel natural, because I naturally look bored anyway. When he says that, Sam laughs, and they have to cut and do a retake because of the smiling thing.

"Talk to each other," the director orders. "It doesn't matter what you say. Just chat with each other."

"Why did you laugh at me?" I ask Sam.

"Give her a hug, Sam, and aim her face toward the camera."

Sam slips his arms around my waist and pulls me close. It's embarrassing with all those people watching, especially my mom, who's sitting on a wooden stool about two inches away. But I don't want Sam to let go either.

"I wasn't laughing at you," he whispers into my ear. "Sorry."

"Can you tell I've never done this before?" I ask him.

He moves away.

"Cross your arms," the director tells us.

We do.

"Sort of," Sam says. "But it doesn't matter. I only started a couple of months ago. You catch on fast."

"Give Sam a noogie," the director says. "And look bored."

I can't knuckle-rub his head without laughing, though. He can't take it without laughing either. I forget all about my mother.

A little while later, after they pat our faces with sponges, the talking part comes. I didn't know we were going to have to talk.

"What do you imagine when you think about the future?" the director asks each of us.

We're supposed to answer, "The future?" As though it's this big question we're worried about. I feel so stupid.

"Don't look at me," I order Sam. "You're going to make me laugh again."

I think he's doing a really good job, but the director isn't happy with his expression. "Brood," the director tells Sam after seven tries. "Let me feel you brood."

"The future?" Sam asks into the camera.

"Help me out here, Grace," the director calls. "Whisper something serious to him."

I don't plan it or anything. It just comes out. "I cut myself once on purpose with a razor blade," I tell Sam quietly, into his neck.

"Beautiful," the director says, when I move away. "Perfect."

My mother takes me to Serendipity's afterward, to celebrate, I guess. I have Sam's phone number in my pocket. He said I could call him anytime. I keep touching it to make sure it's still there.

"Grace," my mother tries, just before my frozen hot chocolate comes. I don't answer her.

Later, while she's waiting for her credit card back from the waitress, she says, "I'm sorry."

Monique

I WAKE UP in the middle of the night, my leg warm and wet, and it takes me a second to figure out I've peed in the bed. The wetness turns cold almost right away, and I'm so tired, I can't even get up to change the sheets. God damn it.

I forget about it until the next morning, when my sister comes by to drop off old baby clothes she got from the rich lady she whores for.

"They're clean," Molly says. "I washed them myself."

"What's this?" I ask. It's a rag doll with no eyes and the yellow hair almost off.

"Oops," Molly says. "That's Ms. Nelly. You can't have her. Caitlin will go ape shit." Ape shit. Only my sister would use that word. "She peed in her new bed the last time she lost Ms. Nelly," Molly tells me.

LIFE IS FUNNY

I try to figure out who I lost last night.

"What's the matter?" Molly says.

I think about telling her about the piss. I think about telling her I'm through with the baby's father for good.

Molly touches my belly. "How are you feeling?"

"Still blowing my breakfast," I answer.

She makes a face. Molly thinks I'm disgusting. And I am.

"When's your next appointment?" she says.

"Tuesday."

She puts her hand on my stomach again. "There's still time to get rid of it, you know," she whispers.

"Fuck you," I whisper back.

The baby's father calls me from his program.

"I thought you didn't have phone time yet," is the first thing I say.

"How's the baby?" is the first thing he says.

"I got rid of it," I lie.

There's this big silence, and I know he's crying.

"Jesus," I hear him whimper after a while. "Jesus." If he were here, he'd be punching me instead. Bastard.

"And I'm moving," I lie again. My heart shifts, like a rock keeling to one side. "I'm moving upstate, and don't try to find me."

He's wailing now. A low pitch, like a ghoul pissed off. I need to vomit.

"Monique. Jesus. Monique. Please." It's aggravating how he says the same damn thing whether he's fucking or punching or crying.

He blubbers about how he's got three months clean now and he's through with his old ways and please please please.

"I probably loved you once," I tell him, because it's true. "But I hope you get fucked in the ass three ways before Sunday and die." Then I hang up.

I am disgusting.

I try going to school Monday morning, but I can't. I end up smoking cigarettes on the handball courts. Ms. Crosky, the tenth-grade tutor, comes out the side door, surprising me. She's supposed to be at the middle school during the day.

"You look lost," she says.

I shrug.

"You look pregnant, too."

I didn't think I was showing yet.

"Fuck off," I say.

"Are you going to drop out?"

She doesn't even know me.

"I asked you nicely to fuck off," I tell her. I'm hoping she'll disappear after that, but she stays put. I get through a whole other cigarette before she says anything again.

"There's a high school in this district that has day care," she tells me. "Maybe you'd be interested."

"Maybe I'm getting rid of it," I say.

"Maybe," she answers.

"Maybe," I say.

If I were really going to move, I'd pack all my stuff and my mother's marbles, and I'd go to Greenland. The only person I'd write to would be Molly, and she'd be forbidden to tell anyone where I was at. I saw Greenland in a movie once. It's nothing but white and blue and cold and people in brown skin coats, dog-sledding to get around. In Greenland you can always see the air thickening out of your mouth and little crystals on your eyelashes, and every second is pure, uncluttered peace.

My mother's marbles would go pretty well there. There's one thousand of them, exactly, all milky clears. They belong somewhere cold, icy. They look like they sprouted right out of a glacier. My mother counts them every Sunday. She dumps them out of a black drawstring bag and counts them over and over.

She was counting them the morning I told her I didn't want to go to my father's anymore. I was seven, and he'd just dropped me back home after our Saturday sleep-over visit. Molly came running out of our bedroom to see what he'd bought me. She hadn't ever even met her dad, and mine wouldn't let me share him with her.

"I don't want to go anymore," I'd told my mother. I felt disgusting.

"I'm counting," she'd answered.

"Don't make me go next week," I said, louder. She didn't look up from her groups of ten.

Molly tugged at my mother's hand. "Monique's crying," Molly had said.

My mother slapped her hand away, and I'd leaped at the marbles, raking my fingers over and through them, scattering the neat piles into hard clicks of rolling glass. My mother grabbed my hair and yanked me across the rough carpet with one hand until the other had put the mess right.

She never even asked me why, and when Molly did, the next Sunday morning, I knew it was too dirty to say.

There's a guy I notice at the prenatal clinic on Fourth Avenue. He's Spanish, and he's wearing one of those white lab coats. He's the one who takes your blood. I notice him because he's looking at me. And because his eyes aren't brown, or green, or even blue. They're white. Frost white.

"What are you staring at?" I ask him, after they tell me the baby's alive and well and don't drink alcohol.

"What are you staring at?" I say again.

He smiles a huge smile. He's got a ton of white teeth.

"What's so goddamn funny?" I spit.

"You," he says, and I want to kill him. "You're trying to look so ugly, and you can't do it because you're so beautiful."

I would have slammed him right then, but the dyed red-head who answers the phone goes, "Ooooh, Hectah, I'ma tell everybody you finally talk to a girl." She looks at me. "You bettah take this good, sweetheart, 'cause Hectah don't play."

While I'm trying to figure out which one of them to pop first, he loses the smile.

"You are so beautiful," he says.

He doesn't mean pretty. I know that because I'm not pretty and because of the tone of his voice. He means I'm beautiful, me, somewhere inside. Asshole.

I haven't shed a tear since I was six, but the next thing I know I'm out on the curb, crying so hard I think it could kill the baby, and he's sitting next to me, going, "You date dark?"

I sleep over at Molly's the next night, my sixteenth birthday. Her dorm room at NYU is the size of a bunk bed laid out on its side, but she's got the walls lined with stack shelves and pull-out drawers and desktops that hinge out and prop flat. Molly's a fucking genius. She got a full scholarship from her grades and SATs and her entrance essay, which was all about how our mom's crazy but mostly on Sundays.

"Happy birthday," she calls, swinging open her door while I'm still way down the hall. She's filled the place with yellow and white balloons and streamers and a little round cake with white and yellow frosting. She makes me open lavender-ribboned presents, one by one. I get a gift certificate for a thirty-minute massage, a videotape on childbirth, a fleece hat topped by three silver bells, a hardcover copy of *A Tree Grows in Brooklyn,* and a bag full of chocolate-covered pretzels.

"You're such a bitch," I tell her, shaking my head to make the bells ring. "You know I can't get you shit like this for your birthday."

"You're welcome," she says, and tries to give me a hug.

I shake her off, but not too hard, because it feels good to have her touch me.

The telephone rings. It's my mother. I can tell by the way Molly's voice gets extra polite. She hands me the phone. I hand it back to her. She hands it back to me.

"You should have told me you were celebrating over there," my mother complains. "I would have come."

"Uh huh," I mumble. She's full of shit.

"What do we need?" she asks.

"Toilet paper and English muffins," I answer.

She owns a hair salon. It's open from eight a.m. to ten p.m., Monday through Saturday. I never see her if I can help it. I make sure I'm out or closed up in my room by nine forty-five and gone all day Sundays.

"Happy birthday," she says. "You can have a free cut and blow dry."

"Dried-up old whore," I mutter, after we hang up, just to hear Molly tell me I'm disgusting.

Hector takes me out for pizza on his afternoon off. No white coat this time. Just those teeth and eyes. He asks me about the baby's father.

"He's a crack addict," I say.

"Did you love him a lot?" His voice is deep, and he has an accent. His eyes are the color of my mother's marbles. I can't understand how a Spanish person can have eyes that look like glass. I can't understand how anyone could.

"How can you see?" I ask him. "It looks like you're blind, or something."

He shrugs. "Did you love him a lot?" he says again.

"Not a lot."

Hector tells me he graduated high school two years ago,

and he's in a nursing program part-time. His father used to beat him up because nursing is for women and fags, but then his father died of a heart attack. The kids in his neighborhood used to jump him until he started carrying needles around and telling people they had AIDS blood on them, and then everybody stopped fucking with him.

"You have it?" I ask him.

He shakes his head. "You?"

I shake mine.

"I thought maybe that's why you're so mad all the time," he says.

He invites me to see his place. The neighborhood is mostly Puerto Ricans. They speak fast Spanish and sneak smirks at me, peppering their words with *puta,* which means "cunt" or "slut" or something.

In front of his stoop, I finally get it. "You prick," I tell him.

"What?"

"You want some white pussy to show off what a goddamn manly lay you are?"

"What?" he says again. I shove him.

"You piece of limp cock." I spit at his feet. A group of guys on the corner start bullshitting louder, laughing.

I shove him again, and he stumbles backward. I stand

there, waiting for him to punch me, to yell, "Monique. Jesus. Monique. Please."

But Hector doesn't move. "You don't have to do that," he tells me. He acts like he can't even hear those guys squawking and screaming over at us. "You're beautiful," he says. "You don't have to do that."

I'm so out of breath and I have to pee so bad by the time I get home I think I might wet my pants, and then I realize I left my keys on the windowsill in my room. Damn it. I start bawling all over again, even though I thought I'd gotten myself under control by the time I'd hit Flatbush Avenue, and then I start cursing myself out for bawling over a prick like Hector. I'm still bawling and cursing while I check for the extra set of keys that's supposed to be hidden behind the garbage cans three stoops down. When there's nothing but old dog shit in plastic Baggies and white packing peanuts stuck to clumps of dirty leaves, I stop bawling and cursing, and I throw the neighbors' cans all over the place instead, pretending they're Hector, and after that I still have to pee worse than anything.

The bawling tries to start up again on the way over to the salon, making me take deep breaths and letting them out with the word *fuck* to stop it, because I'll be double goddamned if I'll let my mother see me cry.

"I need the keys," I say, before I'm even through the door, before that blast of strawberry and fried hair and chemicals hits my nose.

"Again?" she asks as I blow by her and the cash register, the old-fashioned kind made of brass and shiny black button keys and a crank on one side, the kind that nobody but her knows how to use anymore.

"You heard me," I say, slamming the bathroom door as hard as I can to piss off the idiot customers, and my mother's idiot staff, and especially my idiot mother.

After I'm done peeing, I think about how I shoved Hector and how he called me beautiful, and I want to smash the mirror with my fist or with my forehead. But instead I just stick my face under the swan sink fixtures for a while and then dry off with one of the green cotton capes from the stacks piled on shelves over the toilet.

When I come out, a guy around my age is walking toward some woman sitting under a dryer. He doesn't belong here because for one, he has a crew cut, two, he's male, plus, he's under forty.

"Drew," the woman says when she sees him, like she's surprised.

"I locked myself out," he tells the woman.

"Isn't this funny," my mother says, loud, to everyone,

handing me her master ring so I can wiggle off our apartment key.

Nobody answers but me. "Hilarious," I say.

The woman rummages through a leather purse. She's wearing a Rolex you can tell is real, and her suit looks like the kind my sister's boss wears. Expensive as hell. When she hands her Drew kid their key, her sleeve rides up, and you can see a bunch of bruises the color of the sky on a shitty day. And fingerprint squeeze marks all over. The same kind my father used to give me when I was little.

I stare hard, feeling better by the second while she yanks her sleeve down and the Drew kid turns as pink as her nails.

"What happened to you?" I fake whisper, fake polite, just to mess with them, just to be disgusting. "Looks like you pissed somebody off."

The words aren't even half out of my mouth before he whips his head toward mine and goes, "*Fuck* you."

Then his mother's messed-up arm flashes out to smack him, and in one part of a second he starts to jerk away, and he could, only he stops and takes the slap, and then she drops her hand and just sits there, and he just stands there, and the customers and staff are still and quiet, and my mother rearranges the shampoos in the display case, pretending she can't hear or see any of it, and I want to keep on being disgusting, only the bawling starts up again, and I can't help it, and I go, "I'm sorry. Shit. I'm sorry."

Hector calls me four times before I'll talk to him. His messages are calm, quick. "Monique. It's Hector. Please call me back." Each time he calls I want to bawl and I want him to call back and I smash something. A plate, a ketchup bottle, a lamp, another plate. I can't find my mother's marbles.

On the fifth time, the fifth day, I pick up. "What do you want?"

"I want to be a part of your life."

"Where do you get that shit from? Do you watch soap operas?"

"You're real, Monique. I need to be with someone who's real."

"Faggot," I say.

"That's such immature bullshit," he tells me. I roll my eyes at the phone. "You're too smart to do all that," he says. "You don't have to keep doing all that."

"What makes you the goddamn expert?" I ask him.

"What makes you?" he fires back.

"I hate you," I tell him.

We agree to meet at the handball courts at five. I call Molly before I go. "I can't do this," I say.

"Are you crying?" She doesn't have to sound so shocked.

"No," I sob.

"Don't go," she says. "What did this guy do to you anyway?"

"I think I need to see him."

"Okay," she says, really sarcastic. "Then go."

"Will you come?" I ask.

"Now?"

"Please?"

"Monique, I'm at work."

"Bring Caitlin with you."

"To Brooklyn?"

"Please. I need you to meet him."

"I'm not going to be able to tell anything just by meeting him," she argues.

"Yes, you will," I beg. "You're good at that."

"I have a class at eight," she says. "I can't stay long."

The handball courts are empty, as usual, when I get there. While I wait for Hector and Molly to show up, I imagine them taking one look at each other and falling in love. I imagine them dropping to the pavement and fucking right there in front of Caitlin. I imagine Hector with his dick hanging out of his jeans, forgetting my name, and Molly with her skirt hiked up, apologizing and asking me to take Caitlin back to Manhattan for her.

While I'm imagining all this, I feel the Doritos I ate earlier rising to my chest. At first I think I've made myself sick from being so mad at Molly and Hector for fucking on the blacktop, but then I remember I'm pregnant. My knees give out, and in the same second Hector's here, catching me from behind.

"Are you okay?" he goes, and he hugs me hard. When he finally lets go, Molly's walking up, holding Caitlin by the hand.

"Hi," Molly says.

Caitlin is staring at me. "There's a baby in your stomach?"

"Yeah," I say. Caitlin is so small. Her whole face is the size of my palm, practically. I'm going to have one of her soon. God damn it.

"I'm Molly," Molly says to Hector, who looks confused.

"That's my sister," I tell him.

"I'm Caitlin," Caitlin says. "Molly's my baby-sitter, and we took two trains and a bus to get here, and there were men saying bad words to us on the bus. Do you want to hear what they were saying?"

"No," Molly tells her. "I told you."

"I wanted you two to meet each other," I mumble to Hector.

"Did she tell you what happened?" he asks Molly, after a minute.

"I don't think so," she says, crossing her arms and glaring at me.

"She stepped to me last week. Almost knocked me right

on my butt."

"That's none of her business," I tell him.

Molly puffs hair away from her forehead and glares at me some more.

"Why are your eyes like that?" Caitlin asks Hector. "Molly, why are his eyes like that?" He kneels so she can see his face better, but otherwise he ignores her.

"Did you knock her back?" Molly asks him.

"Molly!" I go, loud.

"I don't play that," he says, looking up at me as if I actually matter. "She lays a hand on me like that again, and we're over. I mean it."

Molly looks impressed. So does Caitlin. "They're like little snowballs," she whispers. "How did you do that?"

"Why do you like her?" Molly asks Hector, trying to pull Caitlin off him.

Caitlin shakes Molly away, puts a teeny hand on each of Hector's cheeks, and moves her face as close to his as she can. Their noses bump while she examines his eyes.

"Because," Hector answers Molly, as though that explains everything.

So many things happen before we're even alone in a room together. Hector makes me talk to Ms. Crosky about that other high school. He signs us up for a childbirth class that won't start for four more months. He meets my mother on a Sunday morning and watches her count marbles. "Why do you do that?" he asks her, very politely. "You never can tell," she says. I piss in the bed twice more and don't talk to him about it and don't change my sheets either. We rent that movie about Greenland and watch it with Molly in her dorm room on a borrowed VCR. We eat a lot of pizza, and I try to pick a lot of fights. Sometimes he gets mad at me and has to walk away to cool off, and when he comes back, he makes me listen to him without swearing, interrupting, or rolling my eyes.

It's very hard.

We start off by lying down with our clothes on, stomach to stomach, hugging. He curves himself around the baby bulge and pets my head. I'm already crying, and then I start swearing.

"God damn it, you better not fuck with me, you prick. You better not, or I'll stab you a million times with a dull knife and send the pieces to your mother."

"You don't have to do that," he whispers. "You know you don't have to do that."

"I'm so disgusting," I try to argue, but his hands and his voice and his marble mother's eyes won't let it be true anymore.

"No," he says. "You're beautiful."

Year Four

Eric
Mickey

Molly
Monique
Linnette
Hector
Caitlin
Jackson

Eric

ME AND MS. Hudson was hate at first sight. She always be staring at me like I'm gonna smoke her or some shit. She a English teacher, a white bitch who don't even know I got two thoughts in my head. She be teaching mad boring shit and acting all like she a gift to God. She tell kids get out her room if they be messing, she tell kids who they think they is with they mouth so bad. She give you a A right in the start and then be taking away all kind of numbers on your grade if you don't be doing homework or be raising your hand and kissing booty. She do a paper, look like you could buy on the corner, with bunch of Herbs writing mad boring stories and shit 'bout the school, then they get numbers put to they grade and they back up to a A. Fucking Herbs man, suck they grandma's pussy for a A.

I ain't got a A my whole life. Special ed left my ass back two times. I be lucky they let me go to ninth grade next year. Only reason I be coming to this shit anyway for Mickey. Mickey seven, but he real smart and he maybe could turn something right if he grow up. I be all set to quit, I be cutting to go with Franklin Avenue, smoking weed and lifting watches from Super Mart, then Mickey starts nerving me all these questions like he motherfucking *Jeopardy*. He say, what make the TV get the pictures? What make it go fuzzy? Where water come from? Why Mama like putting a needle in her? 'Bout to kill me with all that 'cause I got to answer him every one, and answering whack questions make you tired. But that Mickey, man, he something else. He fix me Campbell chicken dumpling soups every night, fix up a blunt for me real good when I tell him, he don't never pee my side the bed. He tell all the little bugs he see at school he don't need no daddy 'cause he gots me.

Ms. Hudson can suck my wad, she want, but I got to stay awhile 'cause if I get slammed, all they gonna find be my moms, nodding on Fourth Avenue or fucking some dick promising a white Christmas, then what they going to do with Mickey? They put him in some goddamn house in Queens, they got all kind of other kids beat the shit out of him, mess him, make him fuck they cat. Ms. Hudson want me to shit on her so she could fix me to leave, but I not going nowhere. 'Cause I not at school, I be on Fourth selling shit, lifting shit. School safer. Nobody don't fuck with me 'cause I got fifteen in a month, and I be big. Teachers mostly leave me 'cause I stop messing them. Only that bitch want me out 'cause she think I ain't got two thoughts in my head.

Not so bad, 'specially since Mickey say he want to write words for my pictures, 'cause he like writing and he do it real fine. Every day I takes me paper from some Herb, takes me a pencil, I sits in the back every class, I draws me shit for Mickey. He like all that whack little bug stuff. He like spaceships, he like dinosaurs, he like guns and monsters and Ninja Turtles. He make up mad bad stories and put 'em next to my pictures and we makes us Mickey and Eric comics. He like this basketball dude I drawed, Jordan and Rodman mixed in, and I drawed wings on the dude's legs, so he this superhero or some shit, and Mickey went dope with this dude. Mickey calls the dude Jordman and he make Jordman be all a hero every story. Mickey like those hero types, so I draws all kind of pictures of Jordman doing hero dos, saving little bugs and smoking motherfucker teachers and all kind of good shit. Mickey, he love the shit. He never get tired of making his words to my pictures. He keeps 'em all straight in a notebook I lifted him from Super Mart. He keep that notebook real careful in the place under the bathroom sink.

Mickey be a bad little motherfucker, he say my name
before my moms', which my moms didn't even knowed 'cause
she got that pipe or that needle up her ass so deep she don't
know nothing. She always with the stick, ever since I be small,
but she add the pipe after Mickey got two and Mickey's daddy
shot by a cop for some shit. Mickey and me got to lift cheese
puffs and beers and fruit rolls and chicken dumpling soups
'cause she never keep her check. I lift diapers for Mickey, too,
'cause he not so good at holding his water all the time. He cry
pitiful when he mess up, but I don't yell at him none.

So I all quiet in the back Ms. Hudson's class and she
start talking 'bout some kind of 'signment, and I be notic-
ing, the kids, 'stead of picking they noses, they laughing and
nerving her all kind of questions. She telling how we got to
write a essay 'bout what we likes in a date. What she mean
is, what we likes to fuck, but she don't say fuck, she say date,
and everybody be laughing. She say we write what we wants
but we got to use real words for "fuck" and "tit" and all that,
she fail any motherfucker who write bad words. She give us
the whole period, and we got to start now. Me, I don't write
good, I don't like to write no 'signments, can't remember last
one I writes for nobody. But I be kind of tired of Jordman
today, and I been thinking how I'm gonna help Mickey if he
get older if I not practice the shit some. Sos I write. 'Fore I

knowed it, I write three pages and the bell not even go yet. Here's what I be writing.

First thing you got to have in a female is looks. She got to be fine. This what fine mean. Female can be any color but not white. But her color got to be smooth all everywheres, smooth like the color part your eye. Female got to be tall to my eyebrow. She got to be skinny in the middle and big butt and big chest. But her chest got to be small enough my hand get around each chest, no problems. Butt got to fit her legs right, and her legs got to be big. She got any kind of hair she want. She have good hair, okay, she got bad hair, okay. She got braids, she got extensions, she got color, whatever. It all okay but she can't have no shells. She got to have big eyes, her eyes and her nose and her mouth all got to fit right, she got to have white teeths. I like it when the two front teeths not all the way together. She be extra fine, she got two front teeths a little bits apart. She got to have nice breath, and she got to keep herself clean. That a fine female.

Next thing, she got to be fine on the inside. This what fine on the inside mean. She not doing no drugs. She not even drink beers. But she not no Herb. She just got a brain. She smart, but she don't act smart. She stay in school, she make Bs and Cs and sometimes As, but she not in your face. She like a good time. She like making love, but she only like it with her man. She not making love with all everybody. She don't want to have no babies until she finish high school. But she take care of it. She don't make you wear no hat. She listen what you got to say, and she don't mind you don't feel like saying nothing. She like going to the movie, she like dancing, she like hanging out. Maybe she got a little sister she like. She got a moms and a daddy living at home and she like chicken dumpling soups. She like me.

I looks up when I done, and Ms. Bitch all in my face from all over at her desk. The bell ring. She still on my shit. I crumples up her fucking 'signment, leaves it on the floor. Ms. Hudson can suck my wad, all I care.

My moms at home, all skinny. She trying to sleep. She in the bed.

"Why Mama can't be still?" Mickey be asking me. He like watching her sleeping when she home. He think she funny.

"She catch a nightmare," I tell him.

"Where she at when she catch a nightmare?" Mickey say. "She at the nightmare or she here?"

I don't even knowed what he mean, half the questions he nerving on me.

"I don't know," I say. "Make me up a blunt."

"You all out," he tell me. If I want more, I got to go Franklin Avenue. I got to lift me some shit, hang with the crew. I be tired.

"Mama got some," Mickey tell me. "She got two blunts already done. They in her coat." He bring me 'em. They not fixed up real good, but they do all right.

"When I can have some?" Mickey ask me.

"Not never," I tell him.

We watch my moms. We both hoping she wake up and leave 'fore we tired, 'cause there ain't no other bed.

The bitch tell me I got to stay after class today.

"I didn't do nothing," I say. I makes my face get small. It scare white people when you makes your face get small. But she don't look scared. The bitch laughing at me. She laughing at me the whole class. I can't draw, all that laughing she doing. I try to draw Jordman beating her head on a car, but I be messing up. Then she be reading shit in class. She do that other days, but I never be listening. This time she only read one thing. I listen real good, 'cause she be reading my 'signment. I sees it all wrinkled. She picked it up on me and looked. She be reading it out loud, and everybody be listening. When she done she say it be an A except grammar so bad. She give it a C. She say it the best one in the whole class anyway. She don't say my names. Don't nobody knowed it mine.

"Why you do that?" I be asking her after she make me stay.

She show me my 'signment. It got Jordman and some shit and a fine girl drawed all long the sides. She tell me I draw good. She ask me 'bout drawing.

"They for my brother," I be saying. My heart beating mad fast. I be kind of nervous. "He like saying stories to 'em."

She ask me 'bout Mickey. She ask me what I want to do my life. She talking like she not be hating me no more.

"What you doing?" I say. I be mad. Real mad. She trying to trick me. "Why you picking on me?"

"I'm not picking on you, Eric," she say, real soft. "I'm interested in you." What that mean?

"I always thought you were busy back there," she say. She point to back the room. "I'm glad I finally found out what it was you were doing."

"I ain't dumb," I tell her. She think I be dumb.

"Of course you're not dumb," she say. "But if we don't do something about your schoolwork, everyone's going to think you are dumb, and that's worse than being dumb."

I think I be dreaming. I be in here, catching a dream, or I be in bed, Mickey next by? Teacher be telling me, do I want stay after school, get extra help so nobody think I'm dumb no more. Teacher be telling me I can bring Mickey, if he needs come, too. Teacher tell me think 'bout it, tell her anytime. Teacher tell me she hope I meet that fine girl

I writes about. That bitch, she done tricked me all year. Made me think she waiting on me to smoke her.

"I be coming," I tell her. She smile at me. Not nobody but Mickey smile at me for the longest. She got a little place middle her two front teeths. Damn.

Mickey come with me to the Super Mart so I can lift me shit for after school. Shorty there, lifting gum. He like Big Red. He chew it after he get high. He swallow that shit. He must got it all filling up his insides now. He ever get his stomach cut, they gonna find a big wad Big Red.

"Where you been?" he asking me. I ain't lifted nothing yet. I got to wait till he gone. Don't want him telling nobody I'm no Herb, taking notebooks and shit.

"Around," I be saying.

"Saw your mama this morning," Shorty say to Mickey.

"Suck on your sister's tampon," Mickey say. Mickey so bad.

"Where you been?" Shorty say again.

You shrug, you don't got to answer.

"Take little Mick with us," Shorty say. "We fix him up with some good weed. We let him do all the heavy lifting. Y'all oughta come around more."

"Yup," I lie.

"Why you lie?" Mickey ask me when Shorty gone.

*   *   *

We sit in front the room, Mickey and me, in Ms. Hudson's class. We go three times each weeks after school. Four other kids sit in there, too. They not Herbs. They like me. First, I think they dumb, but they not. We do English and maths. Ms. Hudson help us. She still throw us out, somebody starts messing, she still be mad we use bad words. But she help us. Mickey help us, too, 'cause he read better than us. First, I tell him, don't be showing off none, or they gonna kick your butt. But Mickey, he ain't no showoff. He help us little ways. He act like he don't know he know more than us.

Everybody like Mickey. Everybody like his stories. Everybody like Jordman. Mickey tell me we gonna switch it. He tell the story, then I draw the pictures. This Mickey's first story we dos like that.

Once there was a pretty lady who went with men and had nightmares all the time. The pretty lady had a boy. The pretty lady loved her boy a whole lot, but her nightmares made her in a different place so she wasn't ever with him. Jordman was a man with wings on his feet that made him fly and be a hero. Jordman was real nice and strong and his hands always smelled good, like weed. Jordman took the lady's boy with him everywhere. One day the pretty lady was sick in the street and she was at the nightmare place and she didn't know how to get home. Jordman used his wings to fly around the streets to find her. He found her and flew her to a spaceship. The spaceship was real high. It had a McDonald's in it, and the pretty lady ate french fries. Then she had a bath. Then she ate more french fries and she stopped being skinny. Jordman told her the boy missed her. Jordman flew the pretty lady back down to 301 Third Street. She brought the boy a toy from the spaceship McDonald's. They lived happily ever after.

I drawed mad good pictures for that one, and Ms. Hudson put plastic shit around it so it stay nice. Ms. Hudson say to me, "I wish you wouldn't smoke marijuana, Eric. It's bad for you."

"How you know I smoke?" I say.

"How *do* you know I smoke?" she say. Then she go, "I'm not dumb, Eric." Damn.

She ask me do I want my drawings in her newspaper. She say they good enough, and everybody like 'em. She say they go good in the art section. I tell her I'm no Herb. She say she rather me use my names, but she not make me. I think 'bout it. I lets her put my shit in the paper. I don't lets her use my names.

They takes Mickey and me. We home, sleeping, they comes in the door. They say Mickey's teacher made a call. They say we going to different places. Mickey to a family. Me a group home. I bug. I be screaming all kind of motherfucker, faggot, pieces of shit. They call my moms a ho. I jumps one of them 'cause they making Mickey cry. I tells Mickey I'm gonna come get him. I say to Mickey, don't you worry 'bout nothing 'cause I'm gonna get you. They almost be arresting me, but I tells them call Ms. Hudson. I tells them, she gonna tell you. I sees Mickey take his notebook with him out the place under the bathroom sink.

First night at the group home they be leaving me alone. Second night some brother try to fuck my ass. I tears his nose off. Knock out three teeths. Third night some kids be talking to me. They all right. Fourth day they makes me go to school. Ms. Hudson give me all kind of phone numbers, say she been calling. Say she dos anything to help. Say she make sure I gets to see Mickey. She ask me I all right. She close the door and let me sit.

I calls the numbers Ms. Hudson give me. Those people say they gonna help me get back with Mickey. All of a sudden I real busy. I got to go meets these people. They nice. They don't be thinking I stupid. They say yeah, I got to be with Mickey. Welfare not telling me where he at. Ms. Hudson's crew say I got a right to know. They say all kind of laws being broken.

I say to Ms. Hudson, "Why can't Mickey and me lives

where you at?" She don't answer nothing. I guess she got her own kids. I guess she don't need no more. Also, she white. I can't live with no white bitch.

I eats, I sleeps, I shits. I goes to school. I watch TV. I draws. I practice my English and maths. I waits for finding Mickey. I not talking to Ms. Hudson. I goes after school, but I not talking to her. She don't seem like she notice. She still talking to me.

They say my moms in a program. They tells me she not allowed talk to nobody for a while. I hear Shorty got slammed. I smokes my weed. I waits for finding Mickey. I try to see if I can get with him in my dreams. It worked one time. He say, *How you get here?*

I say, *Fix me up a blunt.*

When they find him, Ms. Hudson go with me to Queens or some shit. I knowed it. Ms. Hudson make me bring new pictures for Mickey to write stories. Her people say one more week they gonna put me and Mickey together somewheres. But then we got to change schools.

Ms. Hudson say, "Why don't you come every day this week? It's our last week." We in the train when she say this. I be trying to act like I not with her 'cause I ain't no Herb.

E. R. FRANK

"Who gonna teach me so nobody think I'm dumb?" I say real quiet.

"You'll have to watch every teacher very carefully," she say. She look right in front her face and don't move her mouth much, like she know I don't want nobody seeing us down. "You'll have to choose someone. You'll have to make the first move."

"Bunch of motherfuckers," I say.

"Watch your mouth," she say. She not so bad.

Mickey live in a real house. First thing I see a pretty lady holding a baby. Don't see no cat nowhere. Lady say hi real nice. Point to some room behind that room. Everything clean. Next thing I see Mickey. He be jumping on a bed with some other bug. He jumping hard, but he ain't got no smile. He jumping like he fix up a blunt for me. Trying real bad, taking it real serious. My chest be mad bugging, my eyes funny. I guess I be kind of crying. Mickey see me. He stop jumping, and he go real still. He be looking at me, and I be looking at him. He get off that bed like he got wings on his feets. He fly straight on my chest. I hug him up tight, like I his mama, or some shit.

He smell so good.

Molly

"I CAN'T DO the assignment," I tell my American Culture and Society professor after class. She's in a rush, scraping papers and books from the desk into her black bag.

"Uh huh," she says.

"I don't have the money."

"It's seven dollars," she informs me, as though that ought to clear things up.

"I don't have seven dollars," I say. It doesn't embarrass me anymore, the way it did when I was younger.

"Why don't you speak with Financial Aid?" she suggests, hoisting her bag onto her shoulder. "Maybe they'll cover the cost."

"Do you think they'd cover my day's pay I'll lose if I go?" I ask politely. "It's about sixty dollars." I'm not trying to be difficult.

She sighs and then actually looks at me for the first time. It's a good thing I decided not to wear my cashmere sweater or leather pants this morning. They don't exactly look like hand-me-downs. She glances at her watch. The next period's students are seating themselves behind me, and their professor stands quietly, but close, waiting for us to get out of his way. Mine starts walking again.

"We'll figure something out," she says, over her shoulder. "I'll let you know what next week."

She forgets, but it's moot because Monique points out the obvious while we're eating Chinese in my dorm room.

"What's the big deal?" she says. "Caitlin's mother would love it if you took her to the Statue of Liberty." She's right. I don't know why I didn't think of that. Usually I think of everything. Lately, though, I've been scatterbrained. Misplacing keys. Putting my lipstick in the refrigerator.

Monique is chewing with her mouth open, probably trying to provoke an insult. It doesn't work. Partly because Hector told me a few weeks ago that the more I keep up our "little patterns," the worse it is for her. Sort of like unintended brainwashing. I don't know how my self-destructive little sister found a guy like Hector, but he is a genius when it comes to her. I think he ought to be a psychiatrist instead of a nurse, but he says he doesn't want to hear about everybody's tragic lives. Just those of the ones he loves.

He is truly a phenomenon. Even without his eyes, he would remind me of Tiresias. The blind wise man. But with his eyes, there's no question. They're so light they're almost transparent. At times they're a milky white. Next to his dark skin and hair, those eyes seem impossible, freakish even. Or saintly, if like me, you tend to lean that way.

"Do you want to come?" I ask Monique.

"With what seven dollars?"

"Caitlin's," I tell her. "Mrs. Anderson always gives me more than I need for trips like this."

"Can Hector come, too?"

"Of course," I say.

She smiles. I'm still not used to seeing her smile. She was just starting to, right after she met Hector, but she stopped again for a long time, after she lost the baby.

"Okay," she says. "We'll come." And then she closes her mouth, for a change.

There are pros and cons to being a part-time nanny. On the pro side, I spend most of my time in luxury. The Andersons have two refrigerators—one for soda and juice only—a bathroom larger than my entire dorm room, a TV my height, and an amazingly comfortable L-shaped leather couch. Also, I have first pick from Mrs. Anderson's discarded clothes, usually worn about twice and only slightly big. I'm allowed to do my laundry at the Andersons' for free and to use the phone as often as I want, as long as I don't call long distance. Which is fine, because there's nobody long distance for me to call.

On the con side, there's a huge amount of cleaning, on top of the baby-sitting responsibilities, and I'm generally expected to put aside my own life at a moment's notice to accommodate the Andersons' emergencies. That's difficult a lot of the time since the Andersons don't seem to understand that I'm trying to put myself through college and can only stay at NYU if I keep up a certain average, which is drastically affected by whether or not I miss an exam or have to forgo studying for one in order to baby-sit so that the Andersons can go to the opera.

I was almost fired last year over not being able to stay an extra two hours.

Normally I would, I'd told Mrs. Anderson. *You know I would.*

I was frantically pulling on my coat and boots. Hector had called me not five minutes earlier.

It's going to be a real problem, Mrs. Anderson had said as I was opening the door to leave, *if you can't be flexible once in a blue moon when we need you.*

My sister is having a miscarriage right now, I'd told her. I was calm. I didn't scream. That's Monique's department. Mrs. Anderson looked as though I'd hit her, though.

What's a miscarriage? Caitlin had asked.

I never heard how Mrs. Anderson explained that one because I left.

Later I got a message from Mrs. Anderson saying that she hoped Monique was recovered and that she was looking forward to my return to work.

I thought your sister was younger than you, she said a few weeks later.

She is, I'd said. *She's sixteen.*

Mrs. Anderson was a little more polite with me after that. I didn't mind, though, because I don't have all that much to do with the parents anyway. It would be bad if I had a kid who was a brat. Caitlin's not. She's too smart for her own good, and she's pretty spoiled, but basically she's a nice little person. Once, before Monique was pregnant and before she met Hector, she found Caitlin and me in Caitlin's favorite playground on the Upper East Side. Even though she claimed to hate kids, Monique would do that every now and then, find some excuse to dig in the sandbox or to push Caitlin in the swing.

This time Caitlin spotted Monique before my sister was even inside the gate. Caitlin started shrieking for Monique to go doubles down the slide.

Please, please, please? Caitlin had begged. I vetoed it because I could smell my sister from about a mile away, and I don't think you should be drunk on slides around little children. So I'd sent Monique back to Brooklyn, and Caitlin had cried.

If I could be small again, Monique told me at the playground's fence, slurring her words and watching Caitlin sob, *I'd want to have a friend like her.*

My professor reads essays out loud in class as examples of what we should be considering when we make our Statue of Liberty visit.

The essays are full of Family and Freedom. Great-grandparents kissing their own tears into the ground, imagining streets paved with gold and opportunity. Persecuted and oppressed great-uncles and aunts rejoicing on crowded boat decks as the sun rises over Liberty's torch. Dreams coming true.

"Taking the time to think about where we came from and how we fit into our community can be both educational and emotional," the professor's saying. "Beginning this journey at a public monument that holds so much meaning for so many can make this one of the most profound educational and emotional experiences you'll have had."

The assumption that her assignment will rock our world amazes me. As if our childhoods were some sort of preparation for this other, more valid existence. As if we haven't already learned the most educational and profound lessons just by having lived our lives.

As soon as Caitlin sees Monique and Hector waiting for us near the ferry ticket window, she drops me like I'm a hot potato. "I'm holding their hands!" she yells, running toward them. "I'm holding their hands!"

I watch Monique watching Hector scoop Caitlin up and swing her around, and while I'm thinking about how good it is to finally see Monique halfway happy, my stomach turns. I try to ignore it as I catch up to the three of them.

"Wipe that grin off your face," I tell Monique, meaning to be cute but somehow sounding grumpy instead.

"Fuck you," she answers. "I wasn't smiling. It was gas."

"Funny." I try again, only this time I sound sarcastic, and then my stomach repeats the first turn, making me wonder if my sunny-side-up eggs weren't cooked enough this morning.

"What's funny?" Caitlin asks.

Hector puts her down and kisses my cheek.

"Monique farted," I tell her.

Caitlin giggles hysterically.

"I did not," Monique protests. "Molly did. Molly's disgusting." Which makes Caitlin nearly fall on her face.

"I *feel* disgusting," I mutter to Monique.

"That's a switch," Hector says. "What's wrong?"

I shake my head.

"I'll get the tickets," he offers, and I hand him money.

"Can I pay?" I hear Caitlin asking as they walk away.

Monique frowns. "What's the matter with you?" she asks.

I'm never like this. I shrug.

"You want a cigarette?" she goes.

"Right."

"They help, sometimes." She pulls a crumpled pack from her back pocket and offers it up.

"I thought you were trying to quit," I say.

"I am."

"I'm just cranky," I tell her, pushing the cigarettes away. "I hate this assignment. I hate that class."

"You sound like me," she says, and my intestines twist, hard. "God."

We watch Hector help Caitlin count her change. He holds the tickets in his mouth so that his hands are free.

"But off the subject," Monique says, "I might get main-streamed or skipped back up to my regular grade."

"No way," I tell her.

"Way." She nods.

"That's great," I say, while this morning's grapefruit juice and toast fight over space. I mean it. *"You're* great."

I swoop on her with a huge hug, which she always pretends to hate, but I know she really loves.

"Fuck you," she says, smiling.

On the ferry a school group of kids around Caitlin's age wears plaid uniforms. They're screaming and racing and shoving each other and huddling in little groups, and Caitlin can't stop staring at them.

"Don't you want to look at the water?" I ask her, thinking that if I just hadn't topped it all off with two strawberry Pop-Tarts, I'd be fine now. Ugh. "Or the statue? Look over there. See how huge it is?"

But she can't take her eyes off those kids.

"What's so great about them?" Monique asks.

"They have uniforms," Caitlin says. "They go together."

"So what?" Monique says.

"I don't go with anyone."

"Bull," Monique tells her. "You're smarter and cuter and

more fun than all of those little uniformed monsters put together."

"Monique," I mutter.

"What?" she says. "It's true."

"Let's not give her a big head."

"My head's not big," Caitlin argues. "My head's regular."

"Maybe if you ask nicely, Hector will put you and your regular head on his shoulders," I suggest. Which she does, and he does.

"I'm going to throw up," I tell Monique.

"Are you pregnant?"

"Please," I moan. She knows I'm an actual, live, in-the-flesh nineteen-year-old virgin. She knows I've always been too busy for men.

"Ugh," I groan. My face feels cold and sweaty at the same time.

"Seasick?" We look at each other, and I can tell she's trying not to laugh.

"It's not funny," I snap.

"I know. I'm sorry," she tells me. "It's not that much longer. Look. We're almost there."

"I hate this assignment," I moan. "I hate that class."

She swings her arm over my shoulders, the way I usually do with her. It feels unsure, angular.

"We've never been on a boat before," she says, as if to explain something. She uses her new, post-Hector, soft voice. It's nice, how she says "we," how her arm warms the back of my neck.

I'm so sick by the time we dock it's all I can do to limp onto land.

"Are you going to throw up?" Caitlin keeps asking.

"Nope," I tell her.

"Who will take care of me if you get really sick?" she says.

"I'm not going to get really sick," I answer. "I'll be fine."

But I'm not fine. There's too long a line for the gift shop's bathroom, so Monique yanks me to the waterside path that moats Liberty, and I puke over the metal railing into the wavelets below.

"I can't remember the last time you spewed," Monique tells me, holding my hair back and then handing me bottled water so I can rinse my mouth.

"The last time was never," I say, gargling and then spitting. "Throwing up was your thing."

"You always brought me a clean towel and a ginger ale ice cube," she remembers.

"Every week," I say.

I poured the ginger ale into the plastic trays each Friday

because I knew she'd need them after she got home from her father's. I don't remember where I'd gotten the idea, but it seemed to help. It took me a lot of years to realize there was a pattern. It took me a lot of years to realize that she stopped being sick as soon as her father disappeared and she didn't have to visit him anymore.

"I'm sorry I didn't know what was going on," I tell her now. My knees are weak, and my saliva is sour.

"You're sorry?" she says, as though we've talked about this a lot and in depth. We haven't. "You've got nothing to be sorry about."

"I should have taken better care of you," I tell her.

I have dreams where I'm standing over my mother, who's stuffing her mouth with marbles. I'm screaming, terrified, *Where's Monique, Mom? Where's Monique!* And my mother just keeps cramming in handfuls of marbles, crunching them between her teeth, glass bits frothing from her lips.

"Jesus," Monique says. "You took incredible care of me. You saved me."

I didn't, though.

"Molly, I'm serious," she tells me. "If it weren't for you, I'd have died."

"I should have done something."

"I'm not kidding," she says. "I would have killed myself."

* * *

We decide that Hector will climb with Caitlin up to Liberty's crown, and Monique will stay with me on the ground. Hector takes my pulse and checks my eyes and my tongue one last time.

"Keep drinking water," he orders. "And if you can find some crackers in the gift shop, eat those."

Monique walks with me around the little island. Seagulls hassle each other over our heads. Liberty looks smaller and greener than I thought she would on her stone pedestal. The New York skyline looks bigger and more colorful. I vomit over the railing twice more.

"Pink," Monique calls out the second time. "Cotton candy pink. What did you eat this morning?"

"Shut up," I tell her. She does, and we keep walking. Slowly.

When we were smaller, we used to spend a lot of time like this. Just being together. Waiting out my mother's weekday silence or Sunday craziness. In our room reading books, or outside, circling Prospect Park on foot. Quiet.

We watch a boy juggle a soccer ball while his littler sister keeps count. He's not bad. She's on 103 when I first notice them. He loses the ball at 110.

"Shit," he mutters when the ball bounces away from him.

"You shouldn't swear, Jackson," the girl tells him, and then I recognize her.

"You shouldn't be so ugly," he tells her back. Monique snorts.

"I know that kid," I say.

"Which one?" Monique asks.

"The girl. She used to do Gymboree with Caitlin. A couple of years ago. Her name is Linnette."

"Well, say hi then."

But I'm not in the mood, and we keep walking instead.

"I used to wish we were twins," Monique announces after a while. "So that you could come with me to my father's, and he would think you were me." When I don't answer, she pulls my arm, so I'll stop and look at her.

"Do you understand what I'm telling you?" she asks.

"Perfectly," I say. She shoves out her chin, trying to make herself look ugly, the way she used to do, before Hector. "You wished we could be each other so that he'd get me sometimes instead of you," I explain for her, so she understands that I understand.

"It was a disgusting wish," she says. "I know it was." She pulls out her cigarettes. "So feel free to hate my guts."

"Don't be insane," I tell her, pulling the pack from her hand and tossing it as far as I can. "I hate *his*."

In the gift shop we see a gang banger snatch candy bars and a T-shirt and shove them down his pants, which are so baggy, he can get away with it. He grabs his loot with one hand and holds on to a younger kid's shoulder with his other hand.

"Can I help you, young man?" a clerk asks the younger kid.

Monique squeezes my arm, afraid that the clerk saw the older one stealing. She's always on the side against the law.

"You mean him," the little one goes, pointing to his big brother, very serious. "Eric's the man."

We settle into a grassy area underneath Liberty's side. I'm not feeling so queasy anymore, but I'm dreading the boat ride back.

"So what are you going to do about your paper?" Monique asks.

"I don't know. Make something up maybe."

"I made up a family tree," she tells me.

Immediately I think of her baby that never was. Her non-baby. How it would look as a tiny leaf hanging down from a dotted line linking Monique and her ex-boyfriend's larger leaves. How it would have a slash through it, indicating death, and no name.

"What family tree?"

"We had to do one for history," she explains. "You know. A genogram."

I remember how Hector whispered to her in the hospital. *It's better this way, you weren't ready, it's better this way, its spirit will come back the next time, when it's ours, the same baby will come back, when everybody's ready, it's okay, it's better this way. . . .*

"So I made something up."

"Uh huh."

She would have had to make it up. My mother is the only relative either of us knows, and my mother is, to put it nicely, off-balance. So as far back as I can remember, I was in charge, all the time.

I would make us do our homework after school, and I'd fix dinner. Macaroni and cheese or french toast or eggs or oatmeal or peanut butter sandwiches with bananas. Our daytime meal was school lunch or day camp lunch, depending on the season. My mother left us just enough money to line our stomachs but not to fill them. Saturdays we bought pizza on Seventh Avenue. One slice each and a shared soda. In the years when Monique was gone at her father's on the weekends, I'd be alone Saturday. I would clean our apartment all day, except for a nap I'd take in Monique's bed.

I washed our clothes at the Laundromat down the block. I made Monique help me. The people there knew us. They would give us their extra quarters. Except for Monique's vomiting after father visits, we never got sick. Ever. I remember one of the few times my mother actually spoke to us. She told us that we weren't allowed to get sick. Ever. I guess it worked.

On Sundays my mother counted marbles. She still does, as far as I know. She keeps them in a small homemade sack, and she pours them out and counts them over and over again all day long. She's done this for my entire life. On Sundays she doesn't answer the phone, and she doesn't eat. We weren't allowed to bother her for any reason on Sundays. If we did, she would yell maniacally or hit us. Once I cut my arm on a broken bottle when I fell outside. We were too scared to bother my mother since it was a Sunday, so Monique bandaged the gash with an old ribbon and tape. I still have a white, bumpy scar.

For years I believed all the mothers counted marbles on Sundays. I thought that when I got to be big and grown-up, I would understand why and I'd count marbles, too. When I realized the truth in fourth grade, that it was just *my* mother, I worried for days over whether or not to tell Monique. In the end I thought she ought to know. When I told her, instead of crying or throwing something or screaming at me, she just rolled her eyes and went, *Duh.*

"Hel*lo*! Anybody in there?" Monique's saying now, throwing a handful of grass at me.

"Sorry," I answer. "I was spacing out."

"Jesus. I was telling you something."

"Yeah. The family tree."

"Forget it," Monique says.

"No. Come on. I want to hear."

"Where the fuck *were* you just now?" she complains. "You looked like Mom on Sundays."

"Fuck *you*," I snap. "I'm sick."

A wave of nausea rises in my throat. I want to stand up over the railing again, but I'm too tired. So I lean forward instead.

"I'm sorry," Monique apologizes. "Okay?"

I fight the nausea until it backs off.

"I'm nothing like her," I say. "Sundays or any other day."

"I know," she agrees. "I'm sorry."

"That was such a shitty thing to say."

"I'm *sorry*."

I watch an ant crossing an island of pebbles for a while, and then I blink and lose it.

"So the family tree," I ask finally. "How did you make it up?"

"I pretended I was Caitlin, and I did one that I thought would fit her."

"What fits her?"

"Her parents are married, together and healthy. Both work in Manhattan. Her father's a lawyer, her mother's a banker."

"That's all true."

"Yeah, but I had to make up everything else. I went back three generations. No divorces, no addiction. I gave her an albino great-aunt just for kicks. I gave each parent a couple of brothers and sisters and the grandparents a bunch. I gave her one pair of identical twins from way back who nearly died of the flu when they were ten but miraculously recovered. Two of her ancestors on her mother's side are true blue *Mayflower* Americans. Her father's side all came over from Europe. They were all poor farmers at first and worked their way up."

"Your teacher must have known it was fake."

"She gave me an A."

I smile.

"It's a great family."

I start to laugh.

"Caitlin got a great life," Monique says.

I laugh harder.

"It's not that funny," Monique says, and then I can't stop. It comes out of me from somewhere hidden and deep, like a fountain or a geyser, soothing the bitter mess of the sick before it, easing the burn and sting.

"It wasn't that funny," Monique complains again, after my laughing fades to hiccups and then to quiet.

"There they are!" we hear Hector call, and I spot him

waving at us and trying to get Caitlin's attention at the same time.

Caitlin's hair is sweaty, and her white T-shirt has a chocolate ice-cream stain on it. She's recognized little Linnette, and they're looking at each other sideways, shy, trying to figure out how to be friends again, probably. A couple of years in the life of a little kid is a long time.

When a Frisbee from the uniformed school group sails over their heads, Hector grabs it out of the air, and everyone at once notices his eyes. That's all Caitlin needs.

In about two seconds flat she has Hector kneeling down so the kids can look up close and see that his eyes are the real thing. I watch Linnette getting trampled until her brother grabs and pushes her forward through the tiny crowd.

"Let her see," he yells. "Let her see!"

"Thanks for staying down here with me," I tell Monique, watching her watch Hector and Caitlin again.

"She's got everything a girl could want," Monique says, while Caitlin bosses Hector around in front of her crowd. He's such a good sport.

"Yeah," I agree.

"Except a sister."

*   *   *

On the ferry back I try to think about my assignment. Try to think about Freedom and Opportunity and Streets Paved with Gold. Immigrants birthing generations' worth of stories. Family trees, branching out, dividing, sweeping into horizontal and vertical shapes that equal whole lives. The thing is, nobody tells you the details. Nobody talks about what those lives were really like. How they were actually formed. Nobody describes sisters holding your head while you puke or cursing you out when you make them fold underwear. Nobody notices older kids stuffing gifts into baggy jeans for younger ones, or brothers showing off soccer juggles and crowd control, protecting and insulting and joking and worshiping with voices that share the same cadence, expressions that share the same secrets. The only ones who know what you know. The only ones who can ever really understand.

I think about how Monique believes I saved her when really she saved me.

I think about what I will write for my professor. That much can be made of metal and stone monuments, but they weigh nothing, compared with my sister's arm across my shoulders for the first time.

Year Five

Gingerbread

Keisha

Drew

DeShawn

Mara

Tory

Nick

Ebony

Grace

China

Sonia

Carl

Mattie

Elaine

Gingerbread

I GOT A round head, and round eyes, and a round nose and little bitty ears, and sunset skin, and they call me Gingerbread because that's what I look like: a gingerbread cookie man, and I don't care. I got hyper blood and bad concentration and I got to take my *riddle-in* every day, but I don't care. I got a crackhead mother somewhere on this earth, or maybe dead, but I don't care because I got my real mama and my real daddy since my little gingerbread face came into this place. My mama is white and my daddy is black, and fools try to make shit out of that, and I don't care.

"You act like you popped right out of a cereal box," Keisha tells me the first week of tenth grade, and I smile my gingerbread smile at her pretty self, and she laughs and laughs the way people do, and I love being here on this earth.

"He's a virgin," my friend DeShawn lets her know, and I don't care.

"So am I, fool. What's your problem?" Keisha tells him, but I see the flicker behind her eye, and I care, because I'm what my mama calls "sensitive." And so is my mama. She had me washing my own clothes and sheets as soon as I turned eleven, and at the time I was mad, and a couple months later I was glad because the joy of a boy was messing up cotton like you've never seen, and that shit isn't for your mama.

"You want to chill later?" I ask Keisha.

She goes, "I have to pick up my cousin right after eighth period. How about later after school?"

And I go, "Cool."

My daddy gets home right when I do, as usual. He trades stocks on Wall Street, and they start at the crack of day and finish the same time as teachers, maybe even earlier.

"I met an important girl," I tell him, and he tosses our basketball to my chest.

"You ditching me?" he asks, and I smile and smile.

He helps me get my homework done first, which is hard because I'm always wanting to get up and look around and tap my pencil on the table and jitter my feet on the floor and sing a tune, and it's hard, but my daddy helps me. Fifteen minutes of math, five of ball out back, fifteen minutes of English, five of ball out back, fifteen minutes of social studies, and I've got a hard-on the size of a baseball bat. Oh, please, Daddy, I hope you can't see that. It's time to go meet Keisha, but I want to jerk off, but then I'll miss her at McDonald's, oh, Daddy, what do I do with this thing, and thinking about Keisha just makes it poke up worse.

"You got money?" my daddy asks, even though he's not supposed to because I get my allowance once a week on Sunday nights.

"I'm telling Mama," I joke him while he throws me ten, and I'm out of there, bumping into my hard-on, praying it down so I can walk the street with my head up. Oh, Keisha, here I come, sweet thing.

The usual crew is there, biting straws and sucking on fries and everybody trying to impress everybody the way we do, and everybody playing and play fighting and making the place hum the way it does wherever we are, and there's Keisha.

"Why they call you Gingerbread?" her friend Mara asks me, and I frame my face with my skinny hands and say, "Why do you think?"

And they all titter off like popcorn, girl-style.

"You want to walk?" I ask Keisha.

She goes, "Yeah," and they all go, "Ooohhh," and I go, "Ooohhh," right back.

And DeShawn goes, "You got your hat, my man?" and Keisha goes, "We're talking, not raining, De*dong*," and they all laugh.

When me and Keisha get away a little bit, she says, "You're real funny," which makes me grin up the world, and in a minute we're dodging cracks and dog shit and baby strollers and stomping on leaves the color of the gym floor, and it's good the way our legs go together.

Pretty soon we're way far away from McDonald's, and there's a playground, and we go in there, and Keisha sits on a tire swing and tips some with her feet. She's got big old boots, the size of my daddy's almost, and when I start to poke with a stick, she tries to hide them up under each other.

"Come on," I say. "Let me see."

"They're too big!" she argues.

I go, "They're big all right. They're mad big, and real cute, too," and she kicks her pretty knees right into me, knocking my butt down, and I roll over and over on playground padding, like an action hero all injured.

I stay there awhile, staring up at the sky, cool blue, like my mama's favorite bowl she calls Fiesta ware, which is like saying party ware in Spanish.

"You could be a model," I say, turning my head to look at her better after a while. "You could be a boot model. A shoe model. Sandals and slippers and—"

"Shut up," she says, but she's laughing, too. So I shut up and just keep grinning at her, checking out that curvy mouth and those cheeks up high on her face and smooth skin, like a new piece of soap, and I feel my dick moving around, and I sit up fast.

"So for real, then," I say, all serious. "What do you want to be one day?"

"President."

"No, for real," I go. "What do you want to be?"

And she goes way soft, "Happy," and then she slips off that tire and climbs up a slide, and I hop myself into a seat swing and push off to a glide.

"You think I'm stupid?" she asks, and I fly high, making the whole thing shake and squeak and rock and creak, and then I jump out far and land in a stand.

"You care what I think?" I'm asking her, and she sit-swooshes down to the ground, and in a minute we're chest to chest except her nose is only as high as my breath.

"You care if I care?" she asks me back.

I'm so busy trying to keep my hands to myself I can't hardly answer, and I think I'm going to pop into a million pieces, each one of them laughing and bouncing all on that playground, and she steps back, and I go, "You want to come over sometime?"

And she goes, "That's fine."

Mama can't ask me about it during dinner because they're at it again next door. The man screams mean to his wife, and my daddy shakes his head, and my mama says, "What a life," and we listen for smashes or crashes, hoping the cops will come again, and they do, and I think of their kid, Drew, who finally got away, a freshman at some ivy school. And my daddy rubs my head, and my mama holds his other hand, and we listen to the clink-clatter of our forks and knives and let out some sighs, and I think I might have a funny round face, but I got a good mama and a good daddy, and I'll take the trade any day.

It's only later, during dishes, Mama asks me about Keisha, and I want to say, *She makes good grades but she doesn't kiss butt, and she's pretty but not stuck up, and she's got the same best friends since sixth grade, and she doesn't ever talk them down, and she lives with her aunt Eva instead of with her mama, and she's got a laugh like a little kid, and behind her eyes, she cries,* only it comes out like "She's mad nice." And we clear the table, and I wash, and Mama dries, and we get into our rhythm, like a dance, or a conversation, or a basketball game, and my mama says,

"Invite her over sometime if you want," and I nod and ask her how she met my daddy, and she starts about how they had their mailboxes next to each other at college, and they used to rap and play and say hey, and she talks over the clatter and rub of plates in a sink and under a towel, and my daddy's pretending to pretend not to listen with his face in CNN, and I start thinking about Keisha, and I know I'm going to jerk off just as soon as I leave the kitchen, and I do, and thank the Lord, Jesus, God, Allah, Buddha, Whoever for making it feel so good.

DeShawn's all in my face today, because he's got it for Mara and wants me and Keisha to do a thing for him, any how, any way.

"Me and Keisha are something special," I let him know, even though I've said it before. We're barely touching the edge of our seats, ready to jet, expecting the lunch bell to ring any second. "You want to get in Mara's pants, you plan it out your ownself."

"'Bread, man, I want to have something special with Mara, too. I'm just saying, help me out," and the bell dings, and we're gone, spinning through the mix of locker slams and sneaker squeaks, hair gunk and perfume-covered girl sweat underneath new leather, canvas, cotton smells. Bodies everywhere, every shape every size and thank you Above for baggy boy pants, and there's Keisha and the crew in the corner stair-steps chomping on Doritos and fruit rolls and peanut butter crackers with a red rectangle knife for flicking at the pigeons when you're done.

"What did you get for number eighteen?" Keisha asks me.

And DeShawn yells, "Isosceles triangle."

And Mara goes, "Nuh uh. It was a trapezoid."

And I go, "Bureaucracies freakazoid wrong and wrong again. Octagon."

And Keisha smiles and goes, "Yeah, me, too," and we just know we're meant to be.

DeShawn goes, "How'd you get that?"

And Mara goes, "Yeah, Gingerbread. How'd you get that?" And what can you do when it's hard enough just to get the answer staying in your seat all at one time with no daddy or basketball or jerking off to get you through?

And DeShawn knows, and he goes, "He can't explain stuff good, y'all know how he is," and pulls my neck with the inside elbow of his arm and shines my gingerbread head, and Keisha starts breaking it down, and I watch, all proud, while she opens up her black knapsack and pulls out her papers and the brick book we got to use for math, and she tells them how you do it, all smart and soft and pretty with those big feet staring right at me just begging for a kiss.

"What are you staring at, Gingerbread?" Mara says.

And they all look up, and Keisha's eyes blush, and I tell Mara, "Your nappy head."

And DeShawn goes, "Don't mess with my girl."

And Mara smacks him on the ear and goes, "Who said I'm your girl?"

And DeShawn does his angel in the manger smile, and while Mara's laughing, Keisha asks me do I want to come over later, and they go, "Oooh," and I grin like a fool.

I use the phone in her kitchen to tell my daddy, and he goes, "You going to get your homework done over there, or are you and me doing it tonight?"

Keisha's already got her books out on the table, next to our soda glasses and a bowlful of chips.

"We're doing it now," I tell him.

And he asks, "Who else is over there with you?"

"Her brother," I tell him, and she rolls her calm, sad eyes because everybody's always thinking you're going to fuck any chance you have.

"Where is he?" I ask when I'm through with my daddy, meaning her brother.

She shrugs and looks mad behind her face and goes, "In the back, in his room," and I want to ask her more, but I don't, and we start trying to do our English, but she's as jittery as me, and we end up all over that kitchen, jumping up for more chips, or pulling open drawers like we lost our mamas somewhere in there, and she does my fortune in my palm, her fingertips tracing mine boings straight into my pants, how does it do that, and I'm squirming like a kid at the dentist.

"You're going to have a long life," she tells me, all soft, and I lean up under the table scared to death she's going to think I'm a pervert and not just falling in love, and she pulls her fingertip along another groove in my skin and goes, "You really are a virgin!"

And I go, "How old am I going to be when I first do it?"

And she throws my hand away like it turned prickly and makes her eyes wide and sighs and goes, "Can't tell you that," and we go back to English but not for long. We predict about Mara and DeShawn, and she tells me Mara likes him, and I warn her DeShawn's a good man but he doesn't keep his dick in his pants for too long, and sometimes with girls he forgets about right and wrong, and he'll get bored fast so Mara better know that, and Keisha tells me they'll be perfect for each other because Mara's the same way, a real good friend and not trying to be bad but sometimes leaving guys mad.

Then I get scared, thinking am I a trifle, does all Keisha want from me is some dick and is she really a virgin or am I going to get used, and I start laughing because the truth is what is a fine woman like Keisha going to see in a cookie man like me and how long have I been a fool, and Keisha says, "What's so damn funny this time?"

And I go, "You like me?"

And she goes, "You like me?"

And I go, "I asked first."

And she goes, "Yeah."

And then I go, "Yeah," and then we sit there and do our English for a while.

DeShawn is worse than my mama, wanting to know every bit of it and he gets worked up when I won't say diddly shit.

"You get into her pants at all?" he's asking me, while we wait for the girls at the movie theater.

"I told you, 'Shawn," I tell him again, "I'm not talking about Keisha like that and we didn't do anything anyway except fuck like wild things on her aunt's kitchen table," which he knows is a lie bigger than God, and he's calling me a mad stupid liar when Keisha and Mara show in all their Saturday night, done-up hair, shiny-lipped, cherry chewing gum breath, barely dry fingernail glory.

We snatch that back row for an alien action love story, and we're hardly over the credits when Keisha bumps my knee with her knee, and first I'm thinking she's making a move on me, and then I see what she sees, which is Mara and DeShawn getting it on.

"Want to leave?" I ask, and we have to crawl all over them, and I'm amazed at old DeShawn because he's got his thing out already, and Mara's moving in on it real steady, and me and Keisha are out in the street quicker than a blink.

"Where should we go?" I say.

And Keisha goes, "We could go to my place," which is what we do, and on the way I pick up her hand, and she lets me, and it makes us all giggly.

"You ever want to do it in a movie theater?" she asks while our legs go together over the cracks and dog shit and by baby strollers and leaves the color of night.

"Naah," I say. And then I go, "Why'd they pay money for a movie if they're missing the whole show for booty?" and she laughs and then stops quick when we get in her door, and there's a little kid watching TV on the floor. Keisha's eyes go mad behind her face, but she stays Keisha calm and goes, "Hey, Tory, where's Aunt Eva?"

And the little kid says all nice, "She's down the street playing cards."

And Keisha goes, "Where's Nick?"

And the little kid goes, "In the back in his room." Keisha

stands there still as a teacher before coffee, biting on her pretty curvy lip, and I go, "What's wrong, Keisha?"

And she looks and looks at the little kid and goes, real quiet, almost like it's to her own self, "Nothing as long as I'm around," and before I can ask what that's supposed to mean, she says louder than anything, "That's my cousin Tory."

"Hey, Tory," I say.

"That's my friend Gingerbread," Keisha tells her cousin, and the little kid's face breaks open and crashes out an ocean of laughing, the way people do hearing my name and seeing my face, and I love being here on this earth.

"You okay?" Keisha asks Tory after a while, and the little girl says yeah.

Keisha looks past the hallway to a closed door, and then that door flies open and a boy-man in the doorway yells, "Tory!"

And Keisha yells, "Nick!"

And the boy-man goes, all grumpy evil-eyed, "Shit," and then that door closes, and Keisha stands froze.

"I'm not going in there," Tory tells Keisha, and I feel dumber than dumb because I don't know what's going on, and Tory goes, "I'm never in there with him." And Keisha goes, "Cool."

"Y'all got some food?" I ask, because the air is thick and

mean, and I want Keisha to smile and the kid to laugh again, and they pull out Lucky Charms, but there's no milk, so we eat it with our hands like chips. I do a drumbeat and throw up the bits and catch them in my mouth, and Tory giggles for more, and Keisha pretends to be bored, and Tory picks out all the purple marshmallows from the pile.

"Why's he always hopping around?" Tory asks Keisha.

And Keisha tells her, "Shush."

And I go, "My brain was born mush, makes me mad hyper."

And Tory goes, "For real? For real?"

And Keisha goes, "Tory, chill."

And then I grab the last purple bit and chuck it in the air, and Tory yells, "No fair."

And I catch it in my hand, not my mouth, and I go, "Tell me why she doesn't like Nick, and you can have it."

"Gingerbread, she doesn't know."

Keisha snaps me sharp, and I get nervous I messed up, and Tory begs, "Give me it."

And Keisha tells her, *"Please."*

And Tory says, "Please, Mr. Gingerbread, please."

And I hand it over and look at Keisha and go, "Peace."

She makes my heart bam and my dick shrink up like a shamed dog when she doesn't answer for a while, but then she smiles. Oh, that Keisha smile.

*   *   *

We do our history project together, me and Keisha and Mara and DeShawn, and it's going all wrong. First it was going to be on Martin Luther King, but then Keisha said if she does one more damn thing on Dr. King, God bless all his work and bless his soul, she will die once and for all. And then it was going to be Harriet Tubman, and Mara and me say same bad, and then my daddy hears it all as he gets closer to our stoop, and he says, "What about World War Two and the black troops?"

Daddy bounces the ball in his good suit, and he tells us all about it and there's a book and a movie documentary and don't forget the library.

"Let's do that," Mara says.

And DeShawn says, "Phat."

And I go, "Yeah."

And Keisha swats me soft and sexy with her fine hand and goes, "Fool."

And I squawk, "What?"

And Mara and DeShawn nod like wise kings when Keisha says, "You never told us your daddy was like that!"

And Daddy grins and grins and steps over us and goes on in, and I play all stupid because I'm happy they like him because that's my Wall Street–working, basketball-playing, homework-helping, get-home-early-and-make-Mama-dinner real man daddy, and thank the Lord, Jesus, God, Allah, Buddha, Whoever for all I got.

So me and Keisha are at the public library looking up the troops, and Keisha's all smiles because she read how a Jew woman back then in those nasty murder camps was about to die a starved skeleton and then thought angels were black-skinned man-looking things because that's who saved her, out of nowhere, picking her up right there in black arms with hundreds more picking up her brothers and sisters from death's dungeon, and she didn't even know people that color lived here on this earth.

"You think God's white?" Keisha whispers in the deep back of the stacks. We're all alone down there, and I want to grab and squeeze, and every time I look at those big old eyes and big old feet, I feel the shake in my knees, so I try to focus.

"First, you've got to ask me if I believe in God," I tell her.

And she pokes out her whole face and goes, "What? You don't?"

And I tap my fingers on the book spines, tap on each letter of each line, tap-tapping.

"Gingerbread?" Keisha says.

And I go, "I don't know." And she's quiet, and I say, "You believe in God?" And over her powder, perfume, hair grease,

I smell the books, old paper, million-year-old tree soot, dusty, like floaty dotted magic air caught in the beam of a film projector, and I just want to grab her, so I tap harder.

"I believe in God except then I don't know why he does things to people," she tells me, and she's got that sad, serious face, that one that makes me stop moving all over the place.

"Why are you so sad?" I whisper, feeling dumber than dumb again. She stays quiet, just looking at me all soft and hard and real, and I want to fix her, hug her all up.

"Was God mean to you?" flies right out of my mouth from I don't know where, and I think I better ask my mama or my daddy because they'll know what I know but can't get, and she shakes her head.

"You're real nice, Gingerbread," she tells me. Then that sad washes all out of her face like the stain out of the TV commercial shirt, and her eyes go sexy and blinky, and the next thing I know she's kissing me with that curvy crazy mouth, and everything goes stiller than I ever knew still, and it's all fine Keisha tongue, lips pulling, clean book dust air, sliding sweet-tart breath, cheek, chin, hard dick, oh, Lord.

"You really a virgin?" she asks me, staying up so close she asks my chest, not my breath, and she's pressing so sexy up against my thing I think I could lose it all over the insides of my jeans.

"Uh huh," I go, and we're down to the carpet strip of floor with all those millions of nice books watching, and oh, Lord, I am on her, she's pressing up, I'm pressing down, wet mouth and warm skin under thin girl shirt, my palm stroking, brushing everywhere, sweaty fingers edging into my pants, crawling to my hard, hard dick, holding, squeezing, pressing, feeling, fingers stop and I want to cry, but she's pulling my hand to her jeans, unzip, panties, elastic, heat, slippery, sweaty fingers pushing mine inside, sliding, gliding, hips moving, one finger, two fingers, rocking, moaning, pulling, pushing, oh, Lord, oh, Lord, beautiful Keisha wet hot pussy fucking my fingers, please, please, please let my dick, and then someone's at my back snatching me up, and Keisha screams, and on her feet so fast, and we run, pants open, shirts off, through the books, the musty dusty tree soot smell, winding, weaving, breathing hard from sex and fear.

I wipe my hand on my jeans before tugging her to me, and we walk quiet, step, step, stepping, no talking, just breathing, no looking, just walking all the way to my stoop. My dick is down, but my chest jumping jacks all over the place, and Keisha holds my hand tight and keeps her mouth still.

We settle in on the second to bottom step, and I tap-tap-tap at her back.

"You think I'm a whore now?" She's trying to be all mad, but I hear her words buck up under a little, and I want to hug her tight, no hard dick, just hug nice, and I put my hand flat on her back.

"No way, Keisha. I think you're beautiful."

"I really am a virgin," she tells me. "I never even did that before."

"Me neither," I tell her.

"It was nice."

"It was real nice."

"I don't feel done." Bang, bang, bang goes the jumping jacks, dick standing up straight, like a soldier.

"Me neither."

"I'll be damned if I get myself pregnant."

"Me, too."

"I'll be damned if it's going to hurt."

"Me, too."

"I'm not ready yet." Dick ducks down.

"But I want it to be you."

Oh, Lord, Jesus, God, Allah, Buddha, Whoever, thank you thank you thank you.

Keisha and Tory eat dinner over lots of times, and their aunt Eva lets them so she can eat over and play cards at her friend's, and my mama and daddy and everybody gets along good.

"You believe in God?" Keisha asks my mama at dessert tonight.

"Keisha, you not supposed to ask that," Tory hisses at her.

"It's okay, Tory," my mama says. "God questions are fine with me."

"You going to burn in hell," Tory whispers.

And Keisha fixes, "You *are* going to burn in hell. Now shush."

And Tory goes, "Shush you back."

And I'm waiting for my mama's answer, and she says, "I'm more interested in understanding why God is so important to people in the first place before I can figure out if God exists."

And Tory thinks awhile about that, and then she goes, "Gingerbread doesn't believe in God."

"I never said that," I tell them all.

"You really going to burn in hell." Tory nods.

And my daddy goes, "You don't believe in God, 'Bread?"

"God isn't any person," I say. "God isn't any old white man watching down over us."

"True enough," my mama mutters.

"He's got all these crazy ideas," Keisha tells on me, but like she's proud, and now they're all looking my way, seeing what am I going to say, and I ping my spoon on a glass and make ringing zings all over the room.

"God's everything all in us and out of us and before us and after us, like blood and air and smells and time and steam off pavement on a rainy hot day and little kids telling stupid jokes, and fire drills, and the sound of a basketball swishing the net, and car alarms and haircuts and locking your keys inside the house," I tumble out, my mouth ding pinging rat-a-tatting nonstop out of nowhere, and I'm feeling dumber than dumb, and Keisha goes,

"See?" and my daddy does the truly craziest thing, just grabs my Gingerbread head and kisses it all up. When my mama starts to giggle, Tory loud whispers, "These people crazy," and Keisha makes her eyes go wide, and she's about to let Tory swallow some hell, but then my mama's joying all out, turns into a belly snort roar, and then there goes my daddy, hee-heeing himself near out of his seat, and Keisha and Tory stare at my white black yellow gingerbread family like we're more mysterious than God, or Whoever.

My mama and daddy make up excuses for Tory to stay inside before good-bye so me and Keisha can kiss and feel on the stoop. I stopped being scared when my dick gets hard every time because Keisha doesn't think I'm a pervert, she just pushes up to grind, and then sometimes we go soft, and it's not all crazy but hugging touching nice like we get to be little babies again, and Lord—DeShawn, forgive me—but Keisha's my best friend.

Sometimes Mr. Screaming Mean Neighbor man waves and says hi, and while Keisha waves back, I pretend I have dust in my eye, but when it's the wife who calls over, I'm more polite, and Keisha doesn't understand because she's never heard them fight, and I don't tell her because her eyes are filled with too much sad already.

Sometimes Tory gets past my mama and daddy's excuses quick, and she gets her little self outside to nag and nerve and pick.

"Why you like her so much?" Tory asks me out here after dinner number nine.

And Keisha goes, "Why *do* you like her?"

And pretends to tie her shoe on that stoop and I go, "Because she's cool, smart, beautiful, doesn't take anything off anybody, and she's mad, whack, stupid sexy fine," and Tory giggle-skips off the steps.

And Keisha hugs me and makes my ear wet when she whispers, "Let's do it soon." And my trusty crazy dick goes zoom, bang, bam, boom.

*   *   *

Keisha and me find a store that's got the hats in the aisle, not behind the counter, and we roll dice to see who's got to buy them, and it's her, and she starts blushing and giggling, and shoving and whining, and then we decide, we'll both buy them. So Keisha adds a toothbrush and a paperback and cough medicine and a bathmat, and all kinds of shit we don't need to hide the hats, and the lady at the counter's like some sort of zombie, and we run out of there, no sweat, no problem, jittery knees, hard dick already, giggly, silly, scared, love.

My mama and daddy are gone to dinner and a show and a party, and it's just me and Keisha in my Gingerbread room with the mess on the desk and the bed all made up nice with 'Bread-washed sheets. I lock the door, and Keisha puts the hats down, and we get all shy and try to hide, but my room's too small, and we end up in a huddle on the floor.

"You sure?" I go.

And she goes, "Yeah. You sure?"

And I go, "Feel this," and put her hand on my jeans over my hard dick.

She laughs and goes, "Well, damn. That's nothing new," and I look at her deep eyes and her big old feet, and then we're kissing, watery tongues, springy lips, tugging, pulling, and we lie down, and she peels off my shirt, and I unbutton her short, pretty mini, and soon we're all skin to skin, warm, sexy, mouth and hands brushing, stroking over tits and ass and stomach, lost, mush brain, heat, curves, sucking, rocking, slipping, swollen, wet, shiny pussy, pushing, pulsing, breathing, moaning, straining thick dick, hat smells like salt balloons, sticky, rolling over aching stiff thing, shy sly fingers, oh, Lord, its tip kissing her melting slit, slide glides in, deep, swallowed, sucked, rocking, aching, bucking, pumping, fucking, oh, Lord, Jesus, God, Allah, Buddha, Keisha, thank you.

Ebony

Eb,

*Back in Rome from Venice. Still doing mostly runway
stuff, but I got some inside pages in* Italian Vogue, *too.
All you see is my lips. Marty knows the three guys on this
postcard, but I haven't met them. Marty says their faces
aren't half as hot as their butts. Figures.*

Peace,
Grace

If this was awhile ago, I'd find China in about half a minute
to show her my mail, but it's not a while ago, and China more
than likely gets whole pages from Grace anyway, so instead
I pushpin those sandy asses onto my little sisters' bedroom

door. Then I take another pin and dig it under my fingernail until blood wells up and drips in a line down to the web of my dark brown thumb.

Bitch, don't do that, I can hear China saying in my head, and I run water over my finger until the juice washes away.

I have to march behind a white boy I blew last fall. Carl. I can't remember what his dick was like because they all run together after a while, but I do remember he was the only one who ever said he loved me right in the middle of it, and I laughed so hard I bit him, and he never even finished. He knows I'm right here behind him because we've had classes together before, and my last name always comes after his, and because the back of his neck turns blotchy the minute I take my place.

I watch China chilling with this Sonia girl behind her, on the other side of the gym. This Sonia girl is one of those brown skin, long skirt, long sleeve types. You never see her whole damn self. China knows her. They ended up with all the same schedule this year, because they're both real smart, but China says this girl's not going to college because females aren't allowed to in her family. Instead she's going to work in her parents' store on Fourth Street until they make her marry some brown skin robe man. China says the girl doesn't mind, but China minds a lot. She thinks it's worse than murder to have a brain and not go to college. She also thinks it's worse than murder to cut yourself sometimes and to suck off anybody who asks. That's why China and I aren't all that tight anymore.

The thing is, I don't do that shit so much these days anyway. For one, it doesn't rush me the way it used to. Not the dicks or the blood, and for another, it gets boring. I found something better a couple of months ago after me and the guy who owns the dance club on Flatbush messed around in his office. He'd gotten all aggravated because I wouldn't do what he wanted, and I'd gotten all aggravated because I used to at least get wet messing around, and that day I didn't even break a tempera-ture. On the way out I saw this number on the wall. 1 900 THE CHAT (FREE FOR FEMALES). I dialed it as soon as I got home, and now talking on the phone is about all I do.

"Hey, little girl," Mike says. "'S up?"

"Hey," I go.

"You clubbing with me Friday, or is your leg broke again?"

"My leg's broken," I tell him. "Where are you going?"

"Trips," he says. "Not too late, though. I got to get the baby from her mother for the weekend."

"Stop calling her a baby," I tell him. "She's almost five."

"That's always going to be my baby," he tells me.

* * *

"Talk to me, sweet thing," Punch says.

"How's work?" I go.

"Busted an old lady looked just exactly like my grandmama with thirteen pairs of size forty-eight men's shorts in her bag."

"You're making that up."

"Wish I was."

"Is Smitty still messing with you?"

"Smitty messing with everybody."

"Are you going out Saturday?"

"You taking me out?"

"You know I'm not. I've got to watch my little brother." I don't even have a little brother.

"When we going to meet, sweet thing? I want to know what you look like."

"I'm fine," I tell him. "That's all you need to know."

"What do young ladies your age like to eat?" Wesley asks me.

"Food," I tell him. "Why? I'm not going out with you."

"I am aware," Wesley says. "My daughter's coming to town, and I'd like your advice on where to take her for dinner."

"Where's she from, again?" I ask.

"North Carolina," he tells me.

"Can you cook?" I go.

"Barely."

"That's too bad," I say. "She'd like it if you cooked."

Mike and Punch and Wesley call me every day. Jones calls less than that, but he's young like me anyway, so I hang up on him a lot. They all have my real number now.

I like older men. They can be the nastiest, if you don't watch yourself, but if you're not talking dirty, you find out quick who's truly just looking for friends. They tell everything. I hear about money problems and mothers-in-law and supervisors and dreams—the real kind that happen when you sleep, not the other kind. I hear about girlfriends and wives and back pain and the time they got a free CD for being the hundredth caller and how they won some spelling bee when they were small and the route they have to take home when the subways are running funny. I help them settle up their disputes and pick gifts and movies and decide whether or not they ought to stick with this friend or that one. My specialty is advice about their kids.

"You ought to tell Amber where babies really come from," I might say. "You don't want her coming up stupid like that."

Or I'll go, "Well, if you stop talking shit about his mother, maybe he'll stop talking shit about you."

They like to flirt with me sometimes, but they keep it clean, and mostly they act real decent.

"What am I going to do when you go off to Harvard?" Wesley complains all the time.

And Punch always says, "You are something else, sweet thing. Your mama and daddy must be puffed up bigger than a marshmallow in the microwave."

Mike sometimes goes, "You know what, little girl. I just really do love you."

"When are you going to tell Mom the truth?" Mattie asks me on the way to school. She means the truth about me and colleges. My mother always planned for me to go to Howard with China, but I didn't even apply. I told her I wanted to stay in New York. I told her I got into NYU, and I did, on probation. That means I'm supposed to get at least all Bs this last semester but I'm barely passing, and I mean truly by the skin of my ass. I thought I'd be in some serious shit when my teachers started calling home, but none of them did. I guess by your last high school year nobody cares that much anymore.

"She's going to bug when she hears," Elaine says.

"Why don't y'all tell her?" I go.

"Are you serious?" Elaine asks.

"Rather her bug on you than on me," I say.

They're twelve and they get straight As. They used to be cute as anything, and now they're coming up pretty. My mom always says they look like our daddy. He never calls them, but they don't care. They don't remember him because he left us a couple of months before they were born. His hands smelled like Slim Jims, and his shoulders under my butt felt like rocks. He flashed silver when he smiled, and he used to do my hair.

"Your daddy's one of the few men who knows hair," my mother would say, and I would be real proud.

I bump into China in the girls' room the last Monday of school. "You hear from Grace?" she asks. We're both trying to wash our hands, but the sinks don't give up much.

"Got a postcard the other day," I tell her, checking me out in the mirror.

"Me, too," China says. "Here." She hands me Mocha Cocoa. It's my favorite shade. It shouldn't look good on both of us, because our skin's way different, but we always did wear the same lipsticks.

"Thanks," I say.

"I leave in August," China goes.

"It's only June," I say.

"I'll miss you," she tells me.

"It's not like we hang anymore," I remind her, sounding like Grace would if she were here.

"I'll still miss you," China says.

I flash off Wesley onto Mike and flash off Mike expecting Punch, but it's someone else on the phone.

"How's my honey?" he goes.

"Who is this?" I ask because I never could recognize his voice. I only hear it a couple of times a year.

"I'm coming to Brooklyn," he tells me.

"Uh huh," I say. "I have a friend on the other line."

"Don't you hang up this phone before we get a plan," he says.

"Why don't you just write?" I go, sarcastic. That shuts him up a minute because he knows I know he never wrote dick, no matter what bullshit he used to shovel.

"I'm serious now. I'm coming to Brooklyn. Thursday. I'm coming for your graduation."

"Does my mom know?"

"This isn't between me and your mama. This is between me and you."

He's not slurring his words, and he doesn't sound all tired, like usual. Maybe he's done drinking. Maybe he means what he's saying, for a change.

"Let's meet up somewhere for dinner, Thursday," he goes. "So we can spend some time before the big day. You name the place."

"Okay," I say. "Fine. Eight o'clock. Bar and Grill on Fourth Avenue."

It's quiet a second, and then he goes, "Well, what do you look like, honey? I don't even have a picture of you."

"I've got real short hair, practically shaved to my head," I lie. "And I'm sort of yellow-colored, and I have extra-long nails, square on the ends, painted silver."

I don't ask him what he looks like because everybody knows he looks just exactly like my sisters.

My mom stares at me over coffee in the morning.

"What?" I go.

"The twins told me."

"Oh."

She sips. I sort of expect her to say some poetry, which is what she used to do, for years, when she was thinking something deep.

"Why aren't you bugging?" I ask, after she stays quiet.

"I am," she goes.

"Oh."

She stretches her hand out over mine and grabs on. "I

thought you knew you could come to me for anything."

She's a good mother. She's smart, and she works hard and always tries to talk to you. She's way better than what a lot of people have.

"I thought you knew that I would help you fix whatever was wrong," she says.

I shrug. I'm not trying to be disrespectful, but truth is truth.

"You can't fix everything," I say.

"Get out," I tell the twins, while they watch me dress.

"Where are you going?" Mattie asks.

"None of your business."

"You have a date?" Elaine goes.

"Get out!"

"This is new," Elaine says, pulling at the tag on a red and white halter.

"You'll rip it," I say, grabbing it away from her.

"You hate your arms," Elaine goes. "Why did you get this one?"

"It goes good with this," Mattie calls, pulling my red shorts out of the closet.

"Y'all get out of here," I tell them.

"Where are you going?" Mattie asks again.

"I'm meeting up with China," I say.

"I thought you said she was a bitch," Mattie says.

"What about Grace?" Elaine goes. "When is Grace coming back?"

"Never, if she can help it," I tell them.

They take turns doing my hair, until it turns out just right.

He's bald, but he's the twins anyway, all over, everywhere. The same hole in the chin, the same high eyebrows, even the same way of sitting, with his shoulders all hunched over his drink.

I slide onto the stool next to him. He doesn't say anything until after I tell the bartender to get me an ice water.

"You want a beer?" he goes. "Let me buy you a beer."

"No, thanks," I say. I wonder if he'll know my voice.

"Oh, you're clean, huh?" he goes.

I shrug.

"All right," he says. "All right. Nothing wrong with being clean."

He waits a while, and then he says, "You want a ginger ale or something?"

I let him buy me a Coke. I keep waiting for him to look around for the daughter with short hair and silver nails, but you'd never know he was waiting for anybody.

"You meeting your man here?" he asks, while I poke at ice cubes with my finger.

"No," I tell him. "I'm just passing time."

"You do have a man, don't you?" he goes. "Pretty thing like yourself."

I shrug. "What about you?" I ask. "You have a woman?"

He laughs and orders another beer. "In a way I do," he tells me, "and in a way I don't." He pulls out a pack of cigarettes, taps one out, and lights up. "What you should better be asking," he says, "is, do I appreciate women."

"Uh huh," I go.

"Well, the answer is yes." He draws on his cigarette and breathes the smoke away to the side. "I live for women." He leans toward me. "Though some women say I live for the drink."

"You have kids?" I ask him. He drops his eyelids half closed and moves in real close, making my skin turn inside out.

"You want to make some, honey?" he whispers.

"Sonia Kabir," they call, and China's brown skin, long skirt, long-sleeve girl steps up for her diploma. "China Kabo," and China steps up. It's going to be forever before they get to Carl and me. I check out the audience, trying to find Mattie and Elaine and my mom in the crowd. I don't see them, but for a second I think I spot my daddy. For a second I think I see his twins' face, and it's crying. But then I blink, and it's just some other man.

What's that? I'd thought maybe he'd ask after we'd ordered.

Just scars, I'd say, feeling air conditioning prickle my arms for the first time in a good long while.

How did you get them? he'd go, all concerned.

I did it to myself, I'd say.

Now what would make you do a thing like that? he'd ask, and I'd shrug. He would get up from his seat across the table and scoot into the bench booth right next to me. He'd put his arm around my shoulder, firm and fatherly.

I was real angry once, I'd say, finally, and he would nod, like he understood.

Year Six

Keisha

Gingerbread

Grace

Sam

Tory

Nick

Gingerbread

Keisha

Drew

Tory

Keisha

"YOUR MAMA'S PREGNANT again," Aunt Eva tells me while I'm reaching for the butter. She's braiding my cousin Tory's hair and gives one rope a tug to keep her still.

"Aunt Cheryl?" Tory goes.

"Are we taking it?" I ask. The butter's cold and won't spread smooth on my toast. It sticks in yellow clumps.

"Mmm-hmm," Aunt Eva says, pulling a plastic barrette out of her man's shirt pocket and clipping it tight to Tory's head.

My brother Nick slides in from his room in the back, opens the refrigerator, and stares inside, like he's forgotten what he's looking for.

"Your mama getting a new baby," Tory tells him.

"His mama *is* getting a new baby," Aunt Eva fixes. She won't look at me.

Nick leans forward, his back curving toward us at the kitchen table. "Gravy spilled in here," he says, and he closes the refrigerator door.

Before Tory and I leave for school, Aunt Eva corners me in the bathroom. But I beat her to talking and go, "Why didn't you tell me last night?"

"Why do you think?" she whips back.

I could argue it, but the truth is, I know where she's coming from. Last night was when I finally told her me and Gingerbread were fucking. I didn't say "fucking," but still. I had to tell it some way because the only secret I ever kept from Eva, the one about Nick, has been smacking at me harder and harder every time I look at Tory. So awhile ago I figured I better make sure I always give up the big things soon. Before they swallow me until I can't speak at all but just let them slap like a wet shoelace that turns to a razor when it's hit you enough.

"Your sixteen-year-old self is doing what?" she said, after I sat her down and brought her a glass of water with a wedge of orange.

"You heard me," I answered, trying not to care if she bugged.

She sipped at her water, calm as you please, and then went, "If you're pregnant, you better tell me straight up."

"I'm not pregnant," I told her.

"You using something?" she asked. "And don't tell me rhythm, or I'll throw you out."

She would never do that.

"Condoms," I said.

"Every time?"

"Every time."

"He give you trouble about that?"

"He's the one who buys them."

She poked at the orange with her pinkie and squeezed up her face. She has a good face, my aunt Eva. It's got lines and freckles and the biggest nose you ever saw. Gingerbread says she looks like some kind of queen Muppet, and she does.

"You have any questions?" she asked me, finally.

"I think I asked them all when I was small," I lied. The untrue part was that I never asked her about Nick.

"I imagine more might have come up now that you're doing and not reading," she said. She can be real sarcastic when she wants.

"Uh uh." I watched her hold the orange into her mouth and suck on it, the way she does. After a long time I went, "You mad?"

"Just don't let me walk in on you," she warned.

"I hear that," I agreed, getting all crawly just picturing it, and she spat that orange right back into the water, laughing herself right into a choke.

Now she's pulling hairs out of Tory's comb and won't look me in the eye.

"Your mama's staying with us for the summer until the baby comes."

"No, she's not," I say.

"Keisha!" Tory's yelling from the hall. "We going to be late!" Aunt Eva doesn't even fix Tory's grammar.

"I thought that's how you might come out," Eva says.

"You promised." My hands go all claws. "You said we'd never take her back!"

"I said you wouldn't have to live with her again," Eva says. She rolls the comb hair between her thumb and index finger. She looks hard at it, like she's searching for bugs or something. "I found a place for you. It's in the country. It's nice."

"The country?" I go. "Uh uh. I'll stay with Gingerbread."

"I don't think so," she says, all tight around the mouth now. She would have said yes yesterday. Damn.

"Keisha!" Tory yells.

"I'll take you!" Nick offers from somewhere.

I push around Aunt Eva to get out of the bathroom.

"Why can't I stay with Linda or Clancy?" I ask, grabbing my bag from the floor by the TV.

"Linda's back on the street, and Clancy is not trustworthy."

I don't know him. I only met him a couple of times, at Christmas, even though he lives somewhere around here.

I head for Tory and the hall. Nick isn't taking her anywhere.

"Not trustworthy?" I go. "Clancy's your brother."

Aunt Eva follows me to the door and pulls on my arm, making me look at her straight. "Then don't you think I know what I'm talking about?"

"You never said anything like that about him before," I say.

"Anything about what?" Tory asks. She turns her back to me so I'll help her pull the braids out from under her jacket.

"You weren't old enough to hear it before, Miss Thing," Eva says back.

"Why does she have to stay here?" I ask. "Why here?" The thing is, I know why.

"It's for that baby."

If Eva doesn't make my mama look out for it, that baby's going to come out more than messed up.

"I'm not going to no damn country."

"Ooohh," Tory goes.

"Any," Eva says. "And don't you bring *damn* into this house."

"I'm not going."

"It's high time you experienced something different. You've never been anywhere."

"So?"

"Going places stretches your soul. You get to see things."

"I see plenty."

"You get to see things differently," she goes. "I'm not playing, Keisha. You get to understand things differently."

"I understand enough."

"You feel different when you go away," she says.

"How do you know?" I ask her. "You've never been anywhere."

"Well, exactly," she tells me, and I'll be damned if she's not about to cry.

Gingerbread hands back Tory's computer pet.

"You've got to feed it," he tells her. "It beeped me silly all morning."

"We getting a new baby," Tory squawks while a pack of her friends pull her away.

"Don't fall out," I tell him quick, before his face goes yellow. "It's not me."

"Better not be Eva," he says, pulling me up close even though we already missed the first bell and we're not even at our school corner yet. He squeezes my behind and starts kissing at my neck.

"It's all messed up," I whisper, even though he's making me hot and giving me those nice chills at the same time.

"You going to cry?" he asks, backing up to get a good look at me. He's never seen me cry. Damned if I'm going to let him see it now. "Did she flip?" I shake my head, but he's not trying to see it. "She did," he goes. "I knew you shouldn't have told her. She flipped, didn't she?" Now he hugs me nice, and I start crying for real because how am I supposed to get through a whole summer without him?

Time is tricky. You have whole months, even years, when nothing changes a speck, when you don't go anywhere or do anything or think one new thought. And then you can get hit with a day, or an hour, or half a second, when so much happens it's almost like you got born all over again into some brand-new person you for damn sure never expected to meet.

Before the day Gingerbread first talked to me, I'd a long time forgotten about laughing, but the second after he said his own name right out loud, I remembered again. When we first started, I asked why he laughed so much, and he said, like it ought to be plain as day, *Because life is funny,* and maybe that's when I for real started to fall in love.

"I have to talk to you," I tell Nick while Eva's out arguing with Workfare and Tory's at After School. Nick swings his legs up and out to fall over the side of his bed so he can sit. I stay at the doorway. One foot in, one foot out.

"You have to leave." He chews his lower lip and eyeballs the floor. "Before my last day of school." If he's out a few weeks before me, I can be pretty sure he'll be gone for good. "You can't come back."

"Why now?" he asks.

"Why do you think?" I say.

"Was a long time ago."

"I was nine the first time," I remind him. "Tory's almost nine." He looks up.

"I never touched Tory."

"You never will."

"Y'all are my sisters."

"You can't come back."

I've been expecting him to argue shit at me. I have a steak knife up in my sleeve. My hand is curled around the tip so it won't slip out.

I haven't thrown more than five words a week to him for

years. I don't know what he does all day. I don't even know how old he is anymore. Twenty-three. Twenty-four, maybe. I know he's all into the *People's Court* on TV and Lucky Charms cereal. He wears hoodies. I don't think he messes with drugs. But looks-wise, he takes after our mama.

He apologized when I was twelve. He was crying. I don't like to remember that. I like to remember the time he spelled and defined "metamorphosis" when my mama was clean. He used her as an example, and he was chewing on the Popsicle stick left over from our lunch that day. When he smiled, his teeth were mad purple.

Aunt Eva gives me ice wrapped in old scarves and head massages when I get migraines. She sits up behind and leans me on her front and tries to make the drilling go away, and usually it doesn't work, but it's good anyway. She tells me stories about how my mama used to do the same for her when they were coming up. Migraines have always been in my family, along with too much using and streeting. But everybody says we each never get more than one bad tendency, so me and Aunt Eva are the lucky ones because headaches don't get you dirty or crazy or doing time or dead.

"I'm not going," I tell her the night before the last day of school.

"Uh huh," she says, rubbing hard.

"Gingerbread's parents said I can stay with them."

"Do they know what the two of you do together?"

"It's not like that's all we ever do," I go. "And you sound like a church lady."

"Well, what am I supposed to say?"

"'Do they know we're fucking.'"

"Keisha! That is worse than disgusting!" But her hands don't stop on my sore head.

We don't say good-bye in some bed, the way it would be if we were a movie. Instead Gingerbread's parents give me a baked chicken dinner and a leather-covered journal with my name in gold on the binding and a box of chocolates for the bus ride, and then they shoo us out.

We meet up with my best friend, Mara, and her man, DeShawn, at McDonald's. Mara gives me a new pair of sunglasses and a baseball hat, and after we chill for a while, they take off, and it's just me and 'Bread in the corner booth.

"Shiny eyes," he whispers, tapping at my palms under the table. I lean out to kiss him and then grab his crazy bitty ears. He sits next to me on the hard orange bench, and I get in his lap, and we end up all chests and necks and arms holding tight.

*   *   *

My mama shows up by the buses lined up and down Flatbush Avenue. She pushes through the crowd to get to me and Aunt Eva.

"When did you talk to her?" I ask Aunt Eva, right as she's going, "When did you talk to her?"

Then we both go, "Shoot."

"Sugar," my mama gushes, shoving her belly right by Aunt Eva. "How you doing, sugar?"

"Who let you out?" I ask.

"Keisha, be nice to me," she says. "I came all the way from Jersey."

"What? You need money?"

She's dressed decent this time, and her hair's done. The last time she looked like she'd been car-washed and thrown in a dryer. The messed-up thing is, she can hide it better than anybody. She could be shooting three needles a day and time things right so nobody can tell.

Mamas and grandmas and aunts and a couple of daddies are tossing bags underneath or shouting for kids to act right. Most of the kids are real small. A lot of them are crying. They look the way I feel. Like they're scared when shove comes to smash, maybe our own don't need us too much.

I give Aunt Eva my biggest squeeze anyway.

"You better call me as soon as that thing pops out of her," I whisper.

"Don't you call the baby 'that thing,'" she whispers back. Then she goes, "You find a good time out there, you understand?"

From the bus window I pull faces and wave at Aunt Eva. I try real hard to ignore my mama, while Aunt Eva and my mama try real hard to ignore each other.

My mama was clean for fourteen months, eleven days, three hours, and I don't know how many seconds when I was eight and nine. She and Nick stayed with me and Aunt Eva that whole time, and she and Aunt Eva not only talked but even laughed some. Mama was afraid to leave the house for most of it, because she was all nerves about picking up, so she bought a dictionary and a thesaurus, and we played with words every day. Her, me, and Nick, all the time.

Veracity, misnomer, solecism, aphony, preterition, hypocrite, utopia.

My teachers started accusing me of cheating and plagiarizing, and then I won an in-class essay contest sponsored by the governor, and the district spelling bee, and then my mother went on a date and didn't come home, not for weeks, and the next time we saw her, she wouldn't look at Aunt Eva and begged me for my spelling bee money, and then I set her dictionary and thesaurus on fire in the bathtub and almost failed fourth grade and forgot to laugh.

A whole group of white people with a bunch of dogs are waiting around in a church parking lot when our bus pulls up. Most of us were busy sleeping the last hour, so we missed our first look at the country, but when I step down onto the gravel in front of a building with a steeple, so white and small and cute I could swear it was just a toy and not even a real church, I get the feeling of soft air and quiet like I never imagined. Even with the bags scuffing on the ground and kids waking up and crying and introductions going on all around and dogs without leashes barking and jumping, it's like I've been living on MTV and they just changed me over to the deep-sea special on the nature channel.

Somebody yells out my name, and I turn around, and there's this man and this woman with wrinkles that would put Yoda to shame and hair so thick and white a baby seal could hide right on their heads. Her eyes are green as a crayon, and his are blue like those trumped-up contact lenses. Their skin is tanned practically to my color, and they walk like professional basketball players: steady and smooth and solid, but with a little attitude poking out somewhere between heel and toe.

"Pleased to meet you," he says, shaking my hand. She leans in and gives me some sugar before I even know what she's up to.

It's another forty-five minutes in the truck with Marge and Tom, who tell me about their two horses, chickens, three cows, a goat, a pig, and a huge vegetable garden. They say not to worry, they didn't want an older kid to do their work for them but just someone they could show a good time and not have to wipe their butts every two seconds. They don't say it exactly like that, but I listen between the lines.

They seem all right, and I've never been in a truck before, which is high up and sort of fun, even though I'm smashed between the two of them and his leg is touching mine and I'm thinking if he so much as tries to look at me funny, somebody's going to have to die, but then again, there's no other place his leg could be what with how crowded things are. And I'm liking the soft air and that I can look in any direction through the truck windows into the dark and the only light I see is from stars up in the sky, and it feels like we could drive right off the edge of the earth because there's no buildings or people or cars or anything anywhere.

"If you're worried you're stuck with just the two of us,"

Marge says right when that's just exactly what I'm worrying about, "our grandnephew is arriving tomorrow morning for most of the summer, too. He's nineteen."

I want 'Bread, is all I'm thinking.

This nephew gets here while Marge is showing me how to collect eggs from under these damn chickens. I'll tell you one thing, I will never eat another chicken again as long as I live because these creatures are nasty-looking, for one, and for two, they act just like every little kid I ever knew and one of them looks enough like a little cousin of mine from the Bronx, I can't hardly keep a straight face about it, which you know has got to be serious. These eggs are the brown kind and have spots, and they're warm, which is sort of amazing and disgusting at the same time and makes me think of my mama with some big brown egg stuffed up inside of her, some brown thing she doesn't even want.

"Hi, Marge," is what interrupts that train of thought, and I could pass out right here when one of the finest boys I ever saw—because as much as I love Gingerbread, he is not fine— walks right up into this dirty old chicken house and gives Marge some sugar.

"Sam," Marge says, "this is Keisha. Keisha. Sam."

He's dark-skinned and has eyes Marge's color, and he is

buff, and if I wasn't so into 'Bread, I'd be a useless puddle by now.

"You ride yet?" he asks me. And I go, "Huh?" because all I can think of is sex. And he smiles, and I'm thinking his white teeth are going to reflect me blind, and he goes, "They've got horses here. You want to ride?"

We don't ride. I'm too scared, so we leave the horses and walk instead. He shows me what's got to be the entire state of Pennsylvania. We walk for hours and hours. I've never walked so much in my life. I've never been on the inside of so much grass and trees and fields and air filled with silky star-shaped seeds swimming by. I never stepped in cowshit or horse-shit, never knew their piles were so damn big, even though if you think on it for two seconds, you know they'd have to be. I never saw tomatoes and cucumbers and corn and basil leaves growing up out of the ground or had round thorn balls get stuck in my socks either. I never knew pigs could be as tame as dogs, even though I read *Charlotte's Web* when I was small and "salutations" was one of the first words me and my mother and Nick found in her dictionary. I never knew that horses smelled like dirt and church lady sweat and hay mixed in or that their noses were softer than a baby's butt. I never knew you can think you understand what it means to live in this world, what it smells like and looks like and feels like on your skin and in your heart, and then, in less time than it takes to get your hair done, you can look up at a whole different sky and realize that all this time you didn't even know who you were, much less stop to wonder.

We sit by a pond where you can hear all kind of hooting movie bird sounds while your ass gets wet on the bank.

"How come you're so dark when Marge and Tom are so white?" I ask Sam. "You adopted?"

"Uh uh," he says. "Marge is my mom's aunt. That's where I get my eyes. My dad's Puerto Rican."

"So where's your mom?"

He shrugs. "Somewhere in Spain, the last we heard."

I don't know what I'm supposed to say after that, so I throw more pebbles into the water. I like to see the circles spread out from the middle. *Concentric.*

"Did you want to come here?" Sam asks me after a while.

"Uh uh," I answer. "My mother's having a baby soon and had to move in with me and my aunt. I hate my mother." I shrug. "So boom. Here I am."

"Where's your father?"

"You must want to marry me," I say, even though I started it, "with all these personal questions."

He smiles and leans back. His T-shirt rides up so I can see his fine belly button with a little trail of hair disappearing down into his jeans. Lord.

"Sorry," he goes. "I just think it's a little weird."

"What?"

"My aunt and uncle having you come here."

"I hear that," I say. Then I go, "What, they never did this before?"

"Nope."

"You want me to leave?"

"I didn't say that."

"You do want me to leave."

"I do not. You don't want to be here."

"Would you?"

We stay still awhile. Then he plucks a grass blade from near his knee and tries to whistle by holding it between his thumbs and blowing into his cupped hands. The sound comes out all squeaky, and he gives up.

"Okay, for real," I say, throwing a pebble at that belly button. "Are you a model or something?"

"Shit," he goes.

I'll be damned. He is a model. He sits up and locks his hands around his legs. "You don't recognize me?" he asks.

"You recognize me?" I sass him back.

"Well, you asked," he says, and his cheeks each go rusty, which I guess is his way of blushing.

"Don't get all embarrassed," I tell him. "What am I supposed to know you from?"

"This perfume commercial," he says. "Some magazine ads."

I shake my head. "Sorry," I go.

He gets rusty again. "Forget it," he mumbles. "Mostly I just go to college."

"You make a lot of money?" I ask.

"Enough," he says.

"You got a girlfriend?"

"You planning on marrying me now?" he goes.

"No." I toss some weeds at him. "I have a boyfriend," I say. "He's my heart." Saying it out like that makes me miss Gingerbread so bad my eyes hurt.

A leaf somersaults toward the pond and then sort of skate-blows over it.

"Well, I got my heart broken awhile ago," Sam says.

"That is hard to believe."

He's not mad. I can tell because he's all smiles, teasing himself right back at me.

"She's way prettier than I am," he says.

"That is hard to believe," I go again.

"You can see for yourself when she gets here," he tells me.

He sits up again, and now I lie back. I watch a cloud change shape in slow motion.

"When she gets here?"

"We're still friends. And Tom and Marge love her. She's coming by on her way back from Italy next week."

"She's Italian?" I never met anyone Italian before.

"No. That's just where models go a lot of times when they start off."

The cloud floats farther away and loses a piece of itself.

"So how'd she break your heart?"

"It's a long story," he says.

"Yeah, well, my secretary tells me I got a little time today," I say.

"Tough."

Night is different here, too. It's quiet of people and engines. It's empty of light after the sun goes down. There're no voices or car alarms or music. There's no TV blue blinking in rows across the way, traffic lights, or neon signs coloring your white wall orange. There're no car brights creeping across your ceiling. There's just this quiet that's different from what happens in class after the teacher screams for it, or after Aunt Eva tells me to hush, or after you set your alarm and turn the light off for bed. It's just this darkness that's different. It's a quiet and a darkness that make you tiny and huge at the same time, make you hear a sort of hum that you never heard before, make you see spots and shapes in the blackness you never saw before, make you think, *What was it like when I was floating around inside my mother?*

I feel real guilty I ever thought anything nasty about Tom because he is one nice man. He and Sam and Marge show me how to brush the horses. I'm too scared of the damn things to ride one yet. The brush has a strap that goes around the back of your hand. You have to move it in circles, and you have to do it hard, and it makes you breathe raggedy and sweat like you'd never guess. They show me how to pick up the horses' feet in my hands, and scrape dirt clumps out of those horse-shoes with a metal tool. They show me how to put on a saddle and buckle the girth, which is like a belt that goes down under that horse's stomach to keep the saddle on and works the exact same way that strap on the brush keeps the brush on my hand. They show me how to hold my palm flat and up, with a chunk of sugar in the middle, for the horse to nibble off.

"You sure you weren't ever on a farm before?" Tom asks the first time I bring in eggs on my own.

"You sure you weren't a comedian before?" I ask him back.

"I hear that," he plays me, and he and Marge look at each other and then laugh like maniacs.

"Do they ever act their age?" I ask Sam.

"Do pigs fly?"

I suck my teeth, trying to act aggravated. "Yours probably do."

On the fifth night I start to cry in my bed in the darkness and quiet. I just cry and cry, and when I get my shit together enough to stop, I turn on my light, walk down the hall, and think about dialing Gingerbread. Only it's way too late for his parents, and nobody said I could call collect there anyway, so I dial Aunt Eva, praying my mama doesn't answer the phone.

"What did they do to you?" is the first thing Eva says.

"Nothing," I tell her.

"You're crying," she argues. "You tell me what happened."

"I just miss you," I go. "I wish you were here."

"You have a headache?" she asks.

"No."

She listens to me sniff for a while.

"Think of a name for the baby," she goes.

"Isn't Mama naming it?"

"Maybe," Eva says.

"Hysteria," I tell her.

"Lord, Keisha, did you call just to torture me?"

"How about Myocardia?" She's trying not to laugh now, and I'm done crying.

"What if it's a boy?" she plays along.

"DeMote," I say, and she snorts.

"Is Mama there?"

"Sleeping in the big bed."

"Where's Tory sleeping?"

"She's got Nick's room now."

"Where's Nick?"

"Still gone," Aunt Eva says.

"Give Tory a hug for me," I say.

She goes, "I love you, Keisha," which starts me crying again, and I can't even say it back.

My first letter from Gingerbread goes like this:

Dear Keisha,

Summer school sucks. My daddy says how you doing? Mara and DeShawn broke up again. I'm teaching Tory basketball. She's pretty good except she's so in love with me she can't hardly hang on to the ball. Jealous? I miss your big feet. I want to make you squirm soon. My heart.

Gingerbread

I keep his letter stuck inside my leather journal under my pillow. I haven't written in the journal yet because for one, I don't want to mess it all up, and for two, I don't hardly know what I'd say.

We're in their vegetable garden, all of us, talking about what movie to rent for tonight when Sam's ex bangs out through the back screened door.

"I'm here," she calls, stopping short on the first wood stump of the wood stump path that goes to the garden.

Lord. I see her picture all the time. And I know her from school. Sort of. She's a few grades ahead of me. She makes Sam look like dog meat. Not that I go that way, but if I did. Lord.

"Where's your stuff?" he asks her, while Tom and Marge step through the tomatoes to give her squeezes.

"The loft," she answers over their shoulders. "Your mom's not coming this year, right?"

"Not this year," Marge says, backing off, and when Tom lets go, too, Sam's ex sees me.

"I'm Grace," she goes. "You're Keisha, right?"

"Hey," I tell her.

"Hi." Then, a second later, she crosses her arms. "Ok*ay*," she says. "I hate staring."

"Yeah, but your fly is open," I lie, and she looks down fast and then rolls her eyes when Marge and Tom and Sam hoot at her and go, *"Ooohhh."*

Walking to the stable, I ask her, "Do we go to the same school?"

"You look kind of familiar," she says. "I dropped out, though." She rubs her eyes. "I had to go to Italy in April."

"I remember you more from when we were smaller," I say. "You were such a bitch."

"I was not. I just looked good. You hung out with that Mara girl and a couple of Jessies."

"Mara and me are still tight," I go. "The Jessies both moved."

"Would you stop staring?"

"What's it like to be famous?" I say.

"She's not famous," Sam goes.

"Nobody knows my name or anything," Grace tells me, like she doesn't care.

"They call you 'the bus bitch,'" I tell her. Her ad is on the side of every damn bus in Brooklyn. "I hear boys shitting every day about chopping off their right arms if they could get with you for an hour."

"You never offered to do that," she complains to Sam, slapping his shoulder. We all three dodge some horseshit, and a ladybug lands on my arm. I make it crawl onto my fingertip so I can watch it better.

"The ninth-grade girls skip their belts a loop," I tell her.

"That ad was a mistake," Grace explains. "The dresser fucked up. Nobody caught it."

"It's fashion now, honey," I tell her.

She sighs and goes, "I hear that."

I throw Sam a look.

"It's not like you invented it," he tells me.

"It's not like she's black," I tell him.

"Racist," he goes.

"Don't start with me," I go back.

"Shut up," Grace orders, and it makes me laugh.

"What?" she asks, all tense.

"Nothing," I say. I put the ladybug in her hair, and she doesn't even notice. It looks like a bright bead on brown velvet. You can smell the horses already, and we're not even inside the barn yet. "Are you going to ride?" I ask her.

"No way." She shudders. "I'm scared to death."

We chill in the hay and watch Sam get Hermes saddled up. I don't know why books talk about hay being so soft you can sleep in it because this shit sticks you like a pricker and itches, too.

"How long are you staying?" Grace asks me.

"About four more weeks."

"Do you like it here?"

How do I answer a question like that? She pulls off her sandals. Her toenails are painted bright blue. Even her feet are fine. "This is a good place," she says. "Marge and Tom are amazing." She wiggles her toes. "And I get away from my mom here."

"What's wrong with her?"

She puts her hands back behind her head, like I'm doing. We watch Sam lead Hermes out of his stall.

"See you," he says. We wave.

"She's just a bitch," Grace tells me. "Plus she's crazy."

"I hear that." I sigh.

Grace waits a second, while one of the cats pounces on my chest. "Also," Grace says, "she's drinking again."

I feel something I haven't felt since I got here. It's a wail at the back of my neck. By nighttime it's going to be slamming all over my whole head.

"She's got a problem with it?" I ask Grace.

"Problem is an understatement," Grace says. Then she looks at me. "You got a problem with that?"

I start laughing. You have to laugh. Life is just funny sometimes. As long as you remember. The cat takes off.

"What?" Grace goes. She sits up, and I keep laughing. "What!" Grace goes again.

"My mother's a dope addict." I giggle. "You got a problem

with that?" She just stares at me with those cut-off-your-right-arm eyes.

"Shit." I sigh, pulling myself together. "You know any good baby names?"

They rent two movies, but damn if my migraine isn't full blown by dessert. I can't see too good, I can't think too straight, and when I try to explain about the ice in the scarves, they all think I've gone foolish. Marge sits on the side of my bed while I'm curled up like the baby inside my mama.

"You want me to call anybody for you?" Marge asks.

"God," I tell her. "I got a list of stuff I need someone to ask him."

"You have a wonderful sense of humor," she tells me.

"Thanks," I moan. "Could you put that hammer down now?"

I can feel her smiling.

"You know, we could make this a regular thing," she goes after a while.

"I'd rather you go ahead and peel off my fingernails," I tell her.

"Not the headaches, Keisha," she goes. "The visits."

Sometimes the slamming turns to squeezing. It's like somebody's got a Keisha head–sized nutcracker, and Lord, are they hungry.

"You could come here every summer. If you want."

"For real," I moan through the pressure. "Why do you even care?"

"It's selfish," she tells me. She doesn't even hold up to think about it. "It's just that Tom and I get lonely. We really enjoy company." She touches my shoulder, light.

"I hate it here," I go. The pain made me.

"That's a damn lie," Marge says. Then she kisses me, real soft on the top of my bursting head, and sits awhile.

The next morning they're all four of them tense, outside. They're butt stuck on the stump path watching the tea-bagged water in a glass pitcher slowly turn brown under the sun. Sun tea, Marge calls it. By lunchtime it'll be done brewing, and she'll throw in mint leaves from the garden.

"I've already checked," Grace is saying, kind of aggravated, like she's said it a million times. "They'll hold my acceptance for the two years."

"What happened?" I ask Sam.

"She's dumping college," Sam says.

"I'm not dumping anything," Grace argues. "I'm just postponing." She squints up from her wooden stump. "I took a two-year contract in Europe," she tells me. Like I'm supposed to know what that means. Then she turns back to Marge and Tom. "Didn't I make sure to take the GED even though I missed the last three months of school? I could have just bailed on the whole education thing, but I didn't."

"Two years' working is a lot different from three months' testing the waters," Tom says. His eyebrows are touching in the middle of his forehead. I never saw them do that before.

"The whole point of the testing the waters," Grace reminds him, close to sarcastic, "was to get signed for real work."

"Well, I wish you'd gotten signed for real work by someone from America," Tom says, "because a few years of the fast life in Europe could make you think you don't need to go to college."

Grace sighs, but Marge beats her to talking. "It's running away from your problems," Marge says. "They'll be here and worse when you get back."

"It's not running away," Grace goes.

"Europe isn't all that great," Sam tells her. "They mess with you over there. Remember what Marty did?"

"I can't believe you guys don't understand this," Grace says. "I thought you'd be excited for me."

"It's good to go away," I tell them. "You get to see things different." They all squint up at me now. "You get to understand things different."

"See," Grace says.

"You feel different when you go away," I warn her.

"Exactly," she goes.

"Do you like Sam?" Grace asks me later. It's just the two of us by the pond. Sam's helping Tom fix part of the fence.

"How come he didn't go to Europe, too?" I ask.

She sighs. "There's this other guy who looks a lot like Sam, only the other guy's taller, and he kisses ass more, and when people want Sam's look, they usually pick the other guy."

"That sucks," I say, feeling bad for Sam.

"Not really," Grace says. "He was never trying to get famous or anything. He hates all that celebrity stuff. All that attention. And he doesn't care about getting away, like I do. He does it for the money, which is what we all say, only Sam really means it."

"Still," I go.

"So do you like him?" Grace asks again.

"You mean like like or just like?"

"Do you want to fuck him?" Grace says. She's using her blue-topped toes to trail a stick in the water.

"Did y'all fuck when you were going out?"

"Don't change the subject." She bugs out on the stick, and it falls into the water without making a sound.

"You're going to be a lawyer after you're done selling your body, aren't you?" I tell her.

"Don't say that," she says. She's not kidding. Her eyes get all watery.

"Sorry," I go. "I was just playing."

She shrugs. "It's true." She sighs. She's the best sigher I ever met. "They pay me a lot of money for the way I look. They pay me more the more skin I show. Do you know how many porn producers have called my agent?"

"Nuh uh."

"Uh." She nods.

"Shit," I tell her. "I'd probably let you take pictures of me butt naked eating a banana and taking a shit if you offered me enough money."

"So do you want to fuck him?"

"Did you fuck him?"

"Yeah," she says. She smiles. Maybe it's the first time I've ever seen her smile. She's beautiful the way you think of beautiful in Bible talk or something. Like an angel or a saint. "He's the only one, though."

"He said you broke his heart."

"Yeah." She sighs.

"Why did y'all break up?"

She shrugs. "I don't know. He's more like a brother, really. You know?"

No.

"I don't want to fuck him," I tell her.

"Really?"

"He's fine," I go. "Don't get me wrong. The boy is fine."

"But?"

"I loves my Gingerbread."

"You really do, don't you?"

I get all happy thinking about his mad letters. Thinking about his bitty ears and his happy laugh. Thinking about seeing him soon. Thinking about fucking him. Grace smiles again, a smirk smile, because damn if she can't tell what I'm thinking.

"You better watch out," I tell her. "Or you're going to crack your face right in two and no Europe's going to give you the time of day."

"You can fuck him if you want," she tells me, laughing. "I wouldn't mind, or anything."

"You're tripping," I tell her.

"I swear," she says.

"Nah," I tell her after a while. "He is more like a brother, you know?"

The good kind. The kind with the purple teeth.

"It's a girl," Aunt Eva tells me while Grace and Sam fold laundry and stack it in piles on the living room couch.

"What? It's a month early," I holler into the phone, and Grace and Sam freeze, with my socks in their hands.

"She's not here yet," Aunt Eva says. "The doctors saw on the whatyamacallit."

I snatch my socks and start folding them myself.

"Any headaches?" Aunt Eva asks.

"One," I say. "Marge rubbed my back and played me whale songs."

"Whale songs?"

"I'm going to bring some for the baby when I come home," I tell her.

"So you still plan on coming home?" Aunt Eva asks.

"What, you don't want me?" I go, and my head gets real heavy and my blood stops, the way it always was after my mama didn't come back and before Gingerbread laughed himself into my face.

"Don't change what I said," she tells me. I hear a mess in her voice. The same mess I heard when the police called that first time to tell us to get my mama out of jail. "I just know that when people leave, they often times find no reason to return." That mess in her voice pulls up my head and pushes my blood to move again. That mess makes me want to reach through the phone somehow and grab her up.

"It's nice here," I tell Aunt Eva, "but I want to come home."

I hear her blow her nose, and I think about how I wouldn't have ever guessed that you might have to go away before you find out how bad you need a person to want you back.

"Well, I need a name for serious now," she complains at me. "Are you going to help me out with that or not?"

"Appaloosa," I say.

"Keisha!"

"Loquatia?"

"God's going to give you your own special room in hell if you don't get it together, girl."

"Irony."

We play Truth or Dare in Sam's room. We speak soft, so we don't wake up Tom and Marge.

"Truth," Sam says to Grace.

"When was the last time you jerked off?"

Lord.

"After dinner," he goes, fast. "Your turn. Truth or Dare?"

"Truth."

"Did you blow Josh?"

"Shit." She rolls her eyes.

"Did you?"

"No." She whips all that hair around to look at me. "Keisha. Truth or Dare?"

"Truth," I go, all nervous, trying to remember the last time *I* jerked off. Yesterday? Or this morning? Lord.

"Are you a virgin?" Grace goes.

"Hell, no."

Grace whips her hair back around again because Sam's saying to her, "Truth or Dare?"

"It's my turn," I tell them.

"Truth," Grace says to Sam.

"Who blew Josh?" Sam asks, fast again.

"Shit." Grace moans.

"Who's Josh?" I ask.

"This guy," they both go.

"Who blew him?" Sam asks.

"Ebony," she says.

"No way," he goes.

"If you tell anyone, she'll kill me, and I'll tell everyone you can't get it up," Grace warns.

"Okay, okay," he goes. "Keisha. Truth or Dare?"

"It's my turn," Grace says.

"Oh, now you care," I tell her. "Dare," I say to Sam.

"I dare you to ride Hermes tonight, double with Grace." Damn.

"No fair," Grace says. "You can't put me in her dare."

"Want to bet?"

*   *   *

Sam leads Hermes out of the stall with me in front of Grace on Hermes's back, which is high and uneven, so some part of my ass is hanging off no matter how I shift around. Grace's arms are around my waist, and we're both scared shitless. The sun is just coming up, so we can barely see, but there's this silver water web shining over everything: the grass, the fences, the ground. Sam leads Hermes and us outside the paddock into the field, and then the silver changes to that gold and brown like you see in old-timey pictures. The sky is mad huge, and the air tastes like fresh parsley.

"Don't be scared," Sam goes.

"I hear that," we both say.

He slaps Hermes on his ass, and Hermes's back slaps at my crotch, and Grace is screaming, and the slapping turns to rocking, and Hermes's feet thumping the ground fills up my ears, and the wet air and earth fill up my heart, and I scream and scream, and then I laugh.

Gingerbread

THE SUN WARMS my arms, and the stoop cools my butt, while I hang on the steps, watching Brooklyn dance by. I pull my ears and put a pebble on my chin and watch the bagel lady and the coffee man settle in, and then my neighbor comes out and I say, "Hey."

And Drew goes, "Hi," and he drops to a step seat in the shade.

We check out bikes and icy trucks and girl couples and the skinny man who sweeps the streets with a brushless broom and yells at the garbage, and we chill still and calm for a while, and then Drew asks me about summer school, which is cool, and about the kids I teach B-ball to in the afternoons, and I ask him when he's going back to college somewhere far away from here. He says in a couple of weeks, he's just killing time, waiting around.

"The final fucking countdown," he tells me, until he's free.

He's a good dude, wired deep, always has been ever since his family moved in when I was eleven. Rich and white and insides real tight, private school, fancy cars but no attitude, just mad sad, crazy quiet. He pulls out his pocket chess set, and we play a few, and I'm wondering how I always do what he felt like all those times the cops pulled up, and then all the times his daddy comes back, and his mama lets him in. This good dude, Drew, he might almost be a for-real man, but he must still be waiting for that shit to end.

"Check," he goes, and I move my king out of the fray, and jiggle my knee and fight the want to ask or tell or say it's going to be okay, but like most times, he's out there, mad far away. Then the checkmate, and we shake, but I moan and groan and play the sore loser to see him smile, and he does, and Tory shows up on her blades, wobbling and bobbling and going, "What's up?"

"Hi, Tory," Drew says, and she tip-crashes her little self over onto the sidewalk, and he helps lift her, which is a trick I taught. She had a crush on me, but now she likes Drew, and really she always knew that her cousin Keisha's my sweetest thing, my Gingerbread head dream.

"Your aunt having her baby yet?" I ask, while Drew packs up his magnet horses and castles and royalty, and Tory says no, but Keisha's mama's as big as the circus fat lady and this week it'll come, maybe.

Drew says, "Later, you two," and disappears next door through his green screen, just breaking poor Tory's little summer heart, but she still waits in case he changes his mind and asks her to marry him.

Then, when she sees he's indoors for good, no more, she flops next to me and whines, "He is so *fine*," and I roll my eyes, and she lets out a big old sigh, and then we sit awhile, and pretty soon she sighs again and moans, "I want Keisha home."

And I go, "You're not the only one," and we slap a soft five, and I say, "I'm just going to sit on this step for the next ten days and wait until she shows her pretty face."

So she nods, and we watch the sidewalks and the tag sales and the trees and think about Keisha and feel the breeze, but it's only a minute Tory can keep quiet, before she complains, "I'm tired of waiting for things," while I ripple my fingers on the brownstone step and tap my foot on her toe stop. "For my baby cousin to be born, for high school to get here, for turning fourteen to make my own money at a real job, for a boyfriend, for Keisha to get home, for you and her to be big enough for a wedding. I've got to wait for everything good. Everything's always waiting."

And I tell her, for an almost-nine-year-old, she's figured

out life pretty clear now, and there's not much else to know, and that makes her smile, the way I like to see people smile, all crooked teeth and crunched eyes, happy.

And me and her and she and I and we sit there thinking our own thoughts, and Tory uses her stubby thumb to spin her skate wheels, so they get to be a purple and orange blur, and I tap on her head, braid by braid by braid, and she gets to laughing, and then she leaves her wheels and grabs my arm, and goes, "Let's play," and I know what she means, and I shake my head and say no way, just to see her beg, and she begs and begs, and I say okay.

Tory clomps back up on her feet and makes me stand tall, and she pulls my arms straight down to my sides, and spreads my fingers wide, and she slides back and looks up, and yells, "Go!" And I try my hardest to stay still and not move, not jiggle, or rock, or tap, or weave, and I try it by watching her big brown eyes looking all over me, and I try and try, and I'm better than I used to be, but I can't help it, I move my tongue inside my mouth and my toes inside my shoes, and I think I've won, but she's too smart and she shouts loud, "You moved! You moved!"

Then we sit all over again, watching four guys and a girl and a moving van block the street and a limo and a rental and a FedEx honking and three bug-eye dogs barking and an old lady hosing at her windows. Then little Tory says, all serious, "I'm sorry, Gingerbread."

And I ask for what, and she's all how maybe that game makes me feel bad and maybe it's mean, and she looks about to cry, and I say, "It's okay, don't worry, if it didn't feel like a fun game, I wouldn't play." And she asks me again all about being a crack baby hyper boy and does it hurt and how long do I have to take that medicine called Ritalin. And I tell her how it could have been bad, but those two who snatched me up for their own on my first daylight helped make it all right because when you have something start you off hard, if you have a good mama and a good daddy or a good anybody to help you through, you can do anything.

Then we watch the roofs and the sky and some floaty leaves flutter by, and Tory says, do I wait for my birth mama to find out where I live, do I wait for my birth daddy to say who he is, or do I wait for my brain to unmush or for people to stop calling me Gingerbread or for high school to be over or for Keisha to get back and come kiss me or to be rich or to not have a bedtime anymore.

And I tell her I have to think on it because it's a lot she needs to know and to come back tomorrow and we'll talk again for sure. And she backs down the stairs holding on to the rails and shaky glides off into Brooklyn, leaving me to watch her like she's my own.

And I feel the warm on my arms and the cool on my butt,

and I see the trees and the leaves and the stacks of books on stoops and the bikes and the dykes, and I think about waiting. Drew's waiting for peace and Tory's waiting for being grown and Keisha's mama's waiting for a baby and Keisha's waiting to come home and I'm waiting to be still, and waiting is everything because when you're done waiting, there's either more or nothing and because it's like the second before someone laughs when you know it will be good and it is, and when they're done, you get to wait some more to hear it again.

Year Seven

Linnette

Eric

Mickey

Linnette

MY MOM ALWAYS used to say there's a whole lot more of real good and real evil in this world than most people could ever imagine possible.

She knows about that kind of thing from her job. My mother's the woman who sits near the witnesses and the judge and types practically every single sound in a courtroom, right down to stutters and swear words. In ten years she's heard more true stories of good and evil than the average person probably hears in a lifetime, TV and gossip included.

She used to talk a lot about it at dinnertime.

"You wouldn't believe the ugliness we had to sit through in court today," she'd say. Or, "I never saw so much kindness inside of one person as I saw this afternoon." Sometimes she wouldn't tell a whole story, exactly, but just certain parts, like how a witness tilted his head when he answered questions, or how someone in the third row cried the whole way through a thirty-three-day trial, or how every single person involved in such and such case seemed to have confusion about the Truth. My mother used to notice that a lot of us can be a part of the same exact thing and have whole different memories of how that thing went. People's emotions and biases mix in and mess up their accuracy, she used to explain to me and my brother. And that's what makes life so mysterious.

Now, though, my mother is pretty quiet at dinnertime. She doesn't set Jackson's place anymore, and it seems like his empty chair across from me is assigned to some invisible hall monitor taking a rest, a strict spirit who won't allow loud talking or much smiling, who might be offended if we seem too happy.

Jackson died two Augusts ago, when I was nine. Now I'm older than he ever was, which was never supposed to happen and which makes me want to cry but not be able to. When I was nine, I believed in God, and the day before Jackson died, I asked my mom and dad why God was making my older brother so sick when Jackson never did anything truly evil in his life. Even though there were lots of times when he would hold me down and pretend to dribble spit right into my face or make me hit myself with my own hand and go, *Why are you hitting yourself, Linny? Why are you hitting yourself?*

My parents said that dying wasn't a punishment on the dead person; it was just that God sometimes takes people when they're young. And I said, *Well, it's a punishment for us, isn't it?* And when my parents didn't answer, I started thinking that maybe God was a lie.

The next day, after I went to get a candy bar from the machine in the waiting room near to the nurse's station, and the machine took my fifty cents without giving me E17, and I came back into Jackson's room, and he was dead, and my parents let me look at him and tell him *see you*, I was pretty sure God was fake, but I still wasn't positive.

A week later I couldn't fall asleep because of hearing my father try not to cry under his pillow and my mother whispering to him the way she whispered to Jackson in the hospital. I tiptoed out of bed and snuck into the living room to the telephone. I crouched down behind the sofa to make sure my parents wouldn't hear me, and then I dialed zero.

Operator. May I help you, please?
I need to make a collect call.
The name of the person who's calling?

Linnette. I tried to whisper, partly not to be heard by my parents but partly to be able to hear them.

The name of the person you're trying to reach?

Jackson.

Number please. Area code first.

I sucked the inside of my cheeks.

I don't exactly know the number.

City or state?

Heaven, please. The operator didn't say anything for a minute, and I thought she had hung up.

Excuse me. Could you repeat the city or state?

Heaven. I said it louder this time, with a little more backbone.

I have a Heavener in Oklahoma.

That didn't sound right to me.

Heaven. The one with God.

The operator took a while to say anything again. I wondered if maybe she was eating.

What is the age of the caller please?

What?

How old are you, miss?

Why did she need to know?

Nine.

Please hold.

I held for a long time. So long that I shifted positions behind the couch and got the buzz in my legs to fade away before she came back.

Miss, Jackson's line is busy at the moment. But if you'd like to leave a message, I'll be sure he gets it.

I tried to think.

Miss?

Well, could I speak to God then?

The operator had a coughing fit, and when she was done, she said, *God's unavailable at this time, miss.*

I don't know how I knew right then, but I did. Maybe it was that the operator's cough sounded more like a laugh. Or maybe it was because I sort of knew all along.

Miss?

Just tell them I called.

I hung up the phone, my palms slippery and my face prickling with disappointment and embarrassment.

Now when my parents ask me about their new plan, with the empty chair listening silently across from me, I can hardly believe it.

"We can't do that," is the first thing I argue.

"We could," my mother says carefully, "if we wanted to." She rakes ridges into her mashed potatoes with the prongs of her fork. "We thought maybe you'd want to." She looks up from her plate and straight at me, the way she used to. "We thought maybe you'd like to have someone else in the family again."

"But it wouldn't be family," I tell them. "It would be fake. A fake family. What's wrong with just us?"

"There's nothing wrong with just us," my father says, folding his napkin into tinier and tinier squares. "That's not the point."

"What is the point?"

My father waits awhile before he answers.

"I guess the point is that Linnette's not comfortable," he finally says to my mom, who drops her fork. The room rings with the sound of it. "If you're not comfortable," he tells me, "we won't do it."

Usually they just go ahead and make decisions on their own. Like when to take vacations and where to go. Like when and how to change around the living room furniture.

"I don't want to," I whisper. My father slowly unworks his napkin until it's spread across his dirty plate. With the creases that came from his folds, it looks like a checkerboard. I glance over at my mother. She has tears ballooning out of her eyes. The only time I've ever seen her cry in my whole life was two Septembers ago, when she got a notice from school saying that Jackson had missed the first fourteen days and would need a note from a doctor to excuse his absence. She sees me looking at her and reaches out to grab my fingers. She's lighter than I am. The backs of her hands are the color of my palms and soles.

"It's okay, Linny," she says. "I'm just a little disappointed, is all."

I wish she would say more, like she used to. I wish she would keep looking at me straight in the eyes and say words the way she used to that made things fit into their place. Made things either easier to understand or magic in how they refused to be understood.

I don't want a new brother or sister, already half grown. I wouldn't want a baby either, if they'd asked. It's not even that I don't want it. I can't. I can't do it.

My father pushes his chair back and circles the table. My mom is still holding on to my fingers. He stands behind her and strokes her hair, cupping her forehead a little first, and then petting backward, slowly.

I never even think all that much about Jackson anymore, much less dream about him, but he comes in my sleep tonight.

Trade you my Milky Way for your Life Savers, he offers.

E17 doesn't work, I tell him, eyeing his candy bar. *How'd you get that?*

Thanks for trying to call, he says, unwrapping his Milky Way and taking the tiniest little nibble off the top.

Don't make fun of me, I warn him.

I'm not, he says. *You want a bite?*

He holds out the chocolate, and I wake up.

It's my father's eyes that are spiderwebbed pink in the morning. My mother has her bottom lip fixed under her top one. That's the look she had the whole time Jackson was sick, and months after, too. I wait until they have their keys out and the front door almost open. They take the same bus to work at first, but then my mom switches at the Port Authority in Manhattan and takes a train two more stops.

"I changed my mind," I tell them.

"What?" my mom says. She looks pretty in her plum suit and suede black heels, even if her mouth is fixed into a flat line.

"Maybe I could try it," I say.

They look at each other.

"Are you sure?" my father asks.

"As long as we can send him away if I don't like it," I tell them.

I expect them both to get on me for being so evil, but instead my father says, "Of course." He looks like he's going to cry again.

"Are you really sure, Linny?" my mother asks.

"Yeah." I nod.

My father pats at his eyes with the heel of his palm. He's wearing a white shirt under his dark suit and cufflinks I made in camp before Jackson died.

"Linny," my mother checks, "what's in your head?"

"As long as we can send him away," I say again.

The thing is, we don't get one. We get two. Eric and Mickey. They look exactly alike, except Mickey is eight, and Eric is sixteen, and Mickey's the one with the shine leaping out of him, and Eric's the one with the hatchet murder face. They're both dark-skinned like me and my dad, and Eric is as tall as a man.

They're supposed to get to our house at three, but they don't show up until five-thirty. They each carry a black knapsack hung over one shoulder.

"You can call me Mr. Wheeler, and this is Ms. Wheeler," my father starts off, after the welfare woman leaves, and we're left feeling stupid in the foyer. My father holds his hand out to Eric, who ignores it the way you would ignore a spot on a wall.

"This is Linnette," my father tells them.

"Hi," I say.

"This a castle?" Mickey says, looking all around and sounding impressed.

"This is a house," my dad says. "I guess it feels big, huh?"

Mickey nods. Eric doesn't say anything.

"Linnette," my mom suggests, "why don't you show the boys their room?"

Jackson's room has two twin beds, now, with blue bedspreads trimmed in cream, two light-colored wooden bureaus, and two light-colored wooden desks. The curtains are blue-and-cream checked, and the floor has a cream rug trimmed in blue. My mother is very good at matching things.

Before, when Jackson lived in here, the room was a mess. Mostly it was filled with balls. All kinds of them. Orange basketballs, red zippered baseballs, swollen softballs, pitted golf balls, sweaty tennis balls, hyper handballs, geometric soccer balls, ugly eye-shaped rugby balls, hard squash balls.

Eric and Mickey are staring at the blue-and-cream room, still holding their knapsacks.

"This was Jackson's room," I explain.

Mickey looks at Eric.

"You can put your stuff down if you want," I tell them.

Eric tosses his knapsack onto the bed nearest the window. Mickey walks over to the other bed and sits on it. He bounces a little.

"My mom says you're from Brooklyn," I try. They don't

answer. "I used to live in Manhattan," I say. "When I was little." I nod toward Mickey. "Like not even his age."

"I'm not little," Mickey says.

"Have you ever been to Montclair before?"

"This called Montclair?" Mickey asks Eric.

"Uh huh."

"We going to stay here now?" Mickey asks.

"Long as you like it here," Eric says, "we stay." He looks at me. "You got a bathroom?"

Eric won't help my mom make a list.

"Don't need nothing," he says. Mickey's sitting so close to him their legs are touching.

"Clothes?" my mother asks. "Notebooks? Shoes?"

Eric shrugs.

"I could have new sneakers?" Mickey pipes.

"Let me see," my mom says, and she leans out from her armchair to grab Mickey's heel. She examines his torn-up Super Mart shoes real carefully, twisting his foot around slow. He starts to giggle. He's a cute giggler. I see a blip of a smile on Eric's face. It makes him look less like a criminal for a second.

My mother leans back and nods. I know she's trying to goof around, but it seems like she doesn't remember how to do it right. Mickey's looking up at her, all eyes and worry lines, to see what she's going to say.

"Absolutely," she says. "Immediately."

"I could get Air Jordans?" Mickey squeaks.

"We'll see," my mom says.

Eric and my dad stay home. My mother writes down the sizes she thinks Eric wears, and she and Mickey and me get ready to go to the mall.

"You not coming?" Mickey says, looking over his shoulder at Eric, who's sitting very straight on his bed by the window.

"'S all right, Mick. I be here when you gets back."

Mickey doesn't like it, though. He goes real quiet and won't smile again. My mother buys him eight pairs of underwear and socks, two pairs of jeans, two pairs of pants, eight T-shirts, two collar shirts, four sweaters, a pair of Air Jordans, a pair of hard-soled shoes, a pair of mittens, a down coat, and a haircut. She buys a couple of things for Eric, too.

"You tell your brother, if his new clothes fit him, we can get more," my mom says to Mickey in the car on the way home. I don't think Mickey hears her, though. His head is hanging to the left, his eyes are closed, and the corner of his mouth is oozing drool.

"What's in your head, Linny?" my mother asks, after a few lights.

"I don't know," I say, poking around in my shopping bags. She bought me a whole new outfit today, including shoes and a pair of earrings. Usually I don't get a shopping trip except in August, to get ready for school, and on my birthday.

"It's just the second day," my mother reminds me. "It's going to feel strange for a while."

Before Jackson died, she'd tell me more. She'd explain it somehow, like a teacher would, or a preacher. I wait a minute, hoping, like I always do, that maybe she'll go on. Fix things with her layers of words, like warm blankets.

"I don't think Eric likes us," I whisper after the hope wears off.

"He just needs to get comfortable," my mom says.

After three weeks he's still not comfortable. He sits in the chair that used to be Jackson's, and it's still the chair that watches over us, keeps us from feeling light. He barely talks, except at night to Mickey, when he thinks the rest of us can't hear.

I spy on them after my parents go to bed. I do it by looking through the keyhole of the bathroom that connects their room to mine. They share the bed by the window. Eric is usually propped by a pillow at his back, knees up. Mickey's usually scootched tight next to him, looking at what Eric's drawing on a tattered pad with a black ballpoint pen. Mickey talks a lot, too, while Eric pulls his pen across the page. I always try to see what's on the pad. Also, I try to hear what they say, but they're too far away, and the keyhole is small.

Sometimes Eric opens the window while Mickey sits cross-legged on the bed, bending over paper and tobacco that he rolls together in his little fingers. When Mickey's done, Eric pulls on the finished cigarette with his mouth and holds the smoke in for a long time before he huffs it out the window. Sometimes he makes smoke rings, which Mickey pokes his fingers through. When the wind is blowing a certain way, the keyhole lets me catch a sniff of something sour and tangy at the same time. I think it's marijuana.

Before, Jackson had bunk beds in that room, crosswise under and over each other. When we weren't fighting, we made forts out of blankets hanging down. We played pirate ship and jail and desert island. Sometimes we'd have a balloon. You couldn't let it touch the top of a bed or a floor or the inside blanket walls, and you could never tap it twice in a row. If the balloon popped, whoever brushed it last had to get hung by the ankles from the top bunk.

Once Jackson dropped me by accident, and I faked that

I was dead. He was so scared he started crying, but when I jumped up, laughing at him, he was so mad he gave me a puffy eye. We weren't allowed to make forts for a whole month after that.

They put Eric in special ed over at the high school. They put Mickey in his regular grade at the elementary school. My father takes Eric on his first day, and my mother takes Mickey. When Eric leaves in the morning, he has his mean face, and he barely even looks at my dad. But at dinner, when my mom asks about how it went, he says, "Was all right."

"We got computers and carpets," Mickey tells Eric.

"You didn't have computers at your old schools?" I ask Eric.

"Linnette!" my father warns.

"What?" I ask.

"Didn't hardly have books in Brooklyn," Eric tells me, sarcastic and ugly.

It snows so much we get to stay home, and my parents can't get into Manhattan for work. My dad asks me and Eric to shovel the walk while he and Mickey build an igloo in the back. Eric purposely waits until I begin, so that he can start at the opposite end of our path, as far away from me as possible. For a while the only sounds I hear are the scrip-scrapes of our shovels against the cement, the shudder of the snow rippling to the side as we go, and Mickey's giggly shouts from the backyard.

"Why don't you like us?" I ask Eric, finally, as we reach each other in the middle of the path. I'm sweating underneath my coat, and my heart is beating fast from exercise and nerves.

Eric just gives me that ice pick look.

"I asked you a question," I tell him.

"Don't like nobody," he says after a while.

"Bull," I argue. "You like Mickey."

He shrugs and stares over my shoulder.

"You don't scare me," I lie. His eyes flash on my face and away again. "And if you're going to stay with us, you better start acting human," I add, scared of what he'll do.

He stands extra still for a second and then takes a deep breath. He swings the shovel up over his head, and for a second I think he's going to bash me with it. Instead he rests it across his shoulders, hands draped over the bar, fluttering from the wrists, and he says, "You know maths and English?"

Eric and I let Mickey sharpen the pencils in my father's electric sharpener. Then Mickey and Eric sit at their desks. Eric has a marble notebook and Mickey has one with cartoon superheroes on the cover. I sit on the bed farthest from the windows, the one that never gets slept in.

"Once upon a time there was a boy without a name," I say. I have to wait a while for their pencils to slow down. "He lived in a big mansion near the ocean."

"What a mansion?" Mickey asks.

"Big house, bigger than this house, but a real house, not no jail," Eric says.

"This boy had a unique talent."

"What a unique talent?" Mickey asks.

"Shut up," Eric tells him.

"What a unique talent?" Mickey asks me.

"Something unusual that you're good at," I tell him. Then I go on. "This boy without a name was good at making himself disappear." I look out the window and think of what to say next. I hear their pencils scratching. I hear one of them erasing something and then blowing the red bits away. From the sound of the blow, I think it's Mickey.

"This boy would make himself disappear when it was time to do the dishes. He would walk into a candy store and make himself disappear just before he would take some candy."

"This boy a stealer?" Mickey asks. He turns all the way around from his desk to look at me.

"Just candy," I say. "Just sometimes, for his sister, when she's sick."

"Yo," Eric grumbles. "Slow down. I can't be going so fast."

Mickey climbs out of his chair and crawls up on the bed next to me. "That boy going to get into trouble?" He lifts up my arm and settles himself into my side. He's warm, and he smells like new shoes.

"I don't know yet," I say. "I'm just making it up now."

"I makes up stories all the time," Mickey tells me.

"Shut up, Mick," Eric says. His voice is sharp. Hatchet man. Mickey pulls my hand down over his head to cover his face.

"You got to check me now," Eric orders. He leans way back in his chair and hands me his notebook. He doesn't know about capital letters or commas or periods. He writes like a little kid. Worse than a little kid. His spelling sucks, too.

"It shit, yo?" he asks me.

"It's pretty bad," I tell him. Mickey peeks out from under my hand. "But I can show you."

Eric works hard. Sometimes Mickey tries to help Eric, but Mickey doesn't know how to explain things very well. He just knows how to do things. I have to be careful because if Eric thinks I'm laughing at him, he'll stand up fast and stomp away, and he won't let me help him for a couple of days.

"He mad," Mickey says whenever I mess up with Eric.

Then Mickey will shake his head, all serious.

"He get mad easy," Mickey will tell me. "But he real soft on the inside."

We do homework, the three of us, after we watch *Oprah* and before my parents get home. We do dictation, too. I always add on to the story of the disappearing boy. First, though, during *Oprah,* Mickey and Eric sit on the sofa eating Campbell's chicken dumpling soup, and I sit in the armchair eating blue corn chips dipped in salsa sauce.

Today Oprah's doing a show on makeovers. Mickey hops up off the couch and walks up close to the TV screen. "That lady look like Mama," he says, pointing to one of the made-over guests.

Eric keeps his face closed.

"Eric," Mickey insists, "that lady look like Mama."

"Nah," Eric finally says. "That lady prettier."

"Mama dead?" Mickey asks Eric. I try not to crunch my corn chip between my teeth because I don't want to drown out Eric's answer.

"Shut up," Eric says.

Mickey climbs back up on the couch and looks at Eric straight in the eyes. Eric stares right back at Mickey, trying to look evil. Mickey smiles at him. "You not mad," he tells

Eric. Then he plops down on his butt and looks over at me.

"My mama dead?" he asks.

"I don't know," I say to Mickey.

"None a your business," Eric mutters.

"Duh," I tell him.

Eric slurps up some dumplings. I've noticed that he eats all the soup part first and then saves the dumplings for last.

"Probably she not dead," Eric says, into his bowl. "Probably she in a program somewhere."

"A program for what?" I ask Eric. He stays quiet, staring at the TV. It's on a commercial now for quick dry nail polish.

"Program is for crackheads to stop using the pipe," Mickey tells me. "Right, Eric?"

Eric glares at Mickey. "You not supposed to tell all everybody that."

"Linny not all everybody," Mickey says. Then he smiles up into Eric's face. "You not mad."

Now Eric glares at me. "She a crackhead and a whore and all kind of nasty shit," Eric tells me. "You heard enough?"

As I watch through the bathroom keyhole, my parents walk in on Eric and Mickey. The tattered sketchpad is open on Mickey's stomach. He's asleep on the bed by the window, and Eric's sitting on the bed's edge, blowing tangy smoke out through the screen. My father takes the cigarette out of Eric's hand. My mother picks up the sketchbook and looks at it for a long time. Eric acts like they haven't even come into the room. He just stays staring out the window. My mother sits on the bed next to him. I keep waiting for her to say something, but I don't think she does. I watch my father head for the bathroom with the cigarette, and before I can move out of the way, he's swinging open the door, hitting me in the face.

On Saturdays Eric and Mickey go to therapy, and I get to have lunch alone with my parents. I used to go to therapy after Jackson died, and so did my parents. But now we eat in a diner once a week instead. I always order a well-done cheeseburger with onion fries and a hot fudge sundae for dessert. Afterward we pick up Mickey and Eric, and my parents switch off taking them out for lunch while I get alone time with whoever's left.

On Sundays we all go out for brunch together. Today the lady who serves my french toast looks at the swollen darkness over my eye, from the bathroom door, and then glances hard and mean at Eric. He glares back at her. When she sets my plate down, I knock over a water glass, right into her black and green apron. She gets soaked.

"Sorry," I tell her, and I give her a blank Eric-style stare.

* * *

When we get home, I follow them into Jackson's room.

"My mom says you draw really good," I tell Eric.

"He draw mad good," Mickey says. "He do pictures for my stories."

"Shut up, Mick," Eric snaps.

"My parents would buy you supplies," I tell Eric. "They'd buy you pads and color pencils and stuff. I bet they'd even help you get into an art class."

Eric keeps his arms crossed over his chest and sits straight, staring out the window.

"Make me up a blunt," he tells Mickey.

"They took it all," Mickey says.

"What's a blunt?" I ask.

Mickey stares at me. A piece of a laugh hops out of Eric's mouth. I can see his teeth. Suddenly he looks more like Mickey than like a murderer.

"She don't know what's a blunt?" Mickey asks him. Now Eric's smiling for real.

"Don't make fun of me," I warn him.

"Weed," Eric says, smirking. "Reefer. Happy smoke."

"Oh," I say. "You mean it's marijuana."

Mickey giggles. "Mari*juana*," he imitates me. "Mari*juana*." He's laughing big now. He's pulling on Eric's knee.

"She talk funny," he snorts. "Eric, she talk so funny!"

"She talk white," Eric tells Mickey, smiling and lying back on the bed. "I be telling you. These niggers talk white."

The word *nigger* makes my ears burn, but Mickey's laughing so hard he falls on the floor.

"Stop it now," Eric orders, but he's giggling a little bit, too. Eric is giggling. "Come on, Mick," he snorts.

Mickey's rolling around on the cream rug with blue trim. He's laughing so hard he's shouting. "Mari*juana*!" he shouts. "Mari*juana*!"

"We've got some news about your mother," my mom says at dinner. Across from me I see the hatchet man come back. He hasn't been around as much lately, but now it's like he never left. Mickey catches it, too. He puts his fork down and looks up, all eyes and worry lines.

"She's finished four months in a program and hopes to finish another eight. She's planning on asking for custody of Mickey after that."

"Do you understand, Mickey?" my father asks.

"No," Mickey says.

"Mama want you back in a while," Eric explains, short and mad.

"What about Eric?" I ask my parents.

He stares straight ahead.

"We're not sure," my mother says to him, reaching out her hand to touch his.

He jerks back and goes stiff as a statue. Only his mouth moves. "Don't matter," Eric tells us. "She not going to be clean that long."

"We going back with Mama soon?" Mickey asks.

"Nah," Eric says. My father rips at his napkin.

"My mama dead?" Mickey asks my parents.

"Not dead," my father finally answers. He gathers a small pile of confetti on his plate. "Just sick."

"Eric," my mother says, sounding like she used to, making my heart take notice with hard little blinks, "I see the whole world come in and out of my job every day. I see everything. I see the good and I see the evil."

Eric's face stays fixed, like a mask.

"Your mother's fighting a war out there. That war got her so young she's been fighting since before you were a thought."

My mom waits a second, while I beg her, in my head, not to stop.

"Evil comes in lots of different ways," she goes on. "It's got your mother by the throat, it's all tangled up inside her, and it's not her fault she can't shake it out."

Eric pushes out Jackson's chair and stands up. I don't want him to go. When he does, my mother will stop talking. She'll disappear again, with him.

"It's not your fault either," my mother tells his back, as he stomps out of the room.

I watch Eric pull on his T-shirt and jeans and shoes. Through the keyhole I see him pull up the covers over Mickey and then walk out the door. From my bedroom window, I watch Eric disappear into the darkness of our quiet street. I set myself up on the stairs in the foyer.

I fall asleep in a nest of blankets, and when I wake up, it's because Eric's leaning down in my face, shaking me.

"What time is it?" I ask.

"Shut up," he says. He pulls me by the shoulder out of the foyer into the living room. His hand is huge and cold. He lets go of me to plop down on the couch. The clock over the TV says it's four-thirteen a.m. I'm not supposed to be alone with him. My parents made that rule on the first day, after the first dinner. That was forever ago, when the snow was just starting, clean and neat, not melted into the little gray lumps lining the edges of our driveway now.

"Where did you go?" I ask.

"Had to get me some weed," he says. He pulls out a

hand-rolled cigarette—a blunt—and a lighter. In a second the end of the blunt glows orange and brown.

"You'll get into trouble," I tell him.

"Shut up," he says, and he takes the blunt from his mouth, holds it in his thumb and first finger, and passes it to me.

"I don't know how," I say.

"Why this shit scare you so bad?" he asks me. "Only make you be relax."

"It doesn't scare me," I lie.

He rolls his eyes. "You is a trip," he says.

"Don't make fun of me."

He tries to hand me the blunt again. This time I take it.

"Hold up," he says. He goes to the kitchen. I hear him fill a glass with water. He comes back and sets the glass on the coffee table.

"It going to burn you. Breathe in and then drink this fast."

I hold the blunt to my mouth and breathe in. It catches my throat on fire, and I choke. It's hard to gulp at the glass, but the water helps. I hand the blunt back to Eric. He sucks without letting his lips touch it and then holds his mouth closed for a long time.

"Who that?" he asks after a while. Smoke curls out from his nose. It makes him look like a dragon. He's staring at a picture of my brother on the mantel.

"That's Jackson," I tell him. It's strange to say his name out loud. It's strange to notice his picture. I forgot it was there. I forgot about his black baseball cap with the orange X, and his gold ball earring in his right ear, and that squint smirk he used to have.

"How long you keep him?" Eric asks. He thinks Jackson was another foster kid. The idea makes me stop breathing for a second.

"Asked you a question," Eric says, leaning back and closing his eyes. I know he's mocking me from that day in the snow.

"Don't make fun of me," I tell him again. He still has the blunt in his hand, and I'm afraid he might burn the couch, so I take it from him and hold it over my water glass.

"Who it be?" he asks again.

"My brother," I say. *That's my brother.* Eric opens his eyes and sits up a little.

"You got a real brother?" I thought he knew.

"He died," I say. Eric takes the blunt back and sucks at it. His cheeks pull in, making him look skinny.

"How old he be when he die?" Eric asks me after a minute.

"Ten," I tell him. *You always sit in his chair,* I want to say.

"He got shot?" Eric asks. I never knew anyone who got shot.

"No," I answer. "He got sick."

"You and him were tight?"

"I don't know."

"Your mama cry?"

I shake my head. *On the inside, like me.* "Mostly my dad," I tell him.

Eric thinks for a minute, and then he leans real close into my face. "You shitting me?" he asks.

It makes me remember something my mother always used to say. *Truth is stranger than fiction, but still, most of us tend to disbelieve truth before we'll question a lie.*

"Nuh uh," I tell him.

"For real, that your brother?" Eric asks me.

"For real."

At the diner on Saturday my father brings it up.

"It's been almost three months," he says.

"What?" I ask. I make designs with my finger on the outside of my Coke glass.

"The boys," my mother tells me. "They've been with us for almost three months."

"What's in your head?" my father asks.

"What's in yours?" I ask right back.

"We want them to stay awhile," he says, "if that's okay with you."

"Eric still smokes weed," I tattle.

The waitress puts my hot fudge sundae smack in the middle of the paper place mat stained with french-fry grease. I feel full now. I'm sick of hot fudge sundaes anyway.

"'*Weed*'?" my father asks.

"And Mickey never sleeps in his own bed. They sleep together."

"No tales, Linny," my mother says.

I pick up the cherry by its stem and twirl it for a while. With its spot of whipped cream, it looks like a snow-capped Christmas ornament.

"Linny?" my father says.

"Okay," I answer.

Mickey and Eric come to the cemetery with us the weekend before Easter. They didn't have to, but they wanted to. It's strange with them here, strange standing near them in the bright sun, watching them stare at Jackson's stone, tiny clusters of new purple crocus pushing up through the grass by their feet.

I don't want them to see my father cry. I don't want them messing up the picture I have in my head of our family. I don't want Jackson, wherever he is, to get confused.

Through the keyhole I can see Eric using his new pad and his new color chalk and oil crayons. I can see Mickey reading from

Eric's marble dictation notebook. I can't hear every word, but
I know what it says anyway:

> *Once upon a time there was a boy without a name. He*
> *lived in a mansion by the ocean. This boy had a unique*
> *talent. He could make himself disappear. He would*
> *make himself disappear when it was time to wash*
> *the dishes. He would make himself disappear when he*
> *wanted to take some candy from the store for his sick*
> *sister. He would make himself disappear when it was*
> *test time at school. He would make himself disappear*
> *when he wanted to hear what other people were saying.*
> *And sometimes he would make himself disappear just*
> *for the fun of disappearing. . . .*

I watch for a while, and then I see Eric tear out the drawing
from its pad, stand up from the bed, and walk toward me.

"Move," Eric orders, through the keyhole, and I do, while
he opens the door.

His hands and T-shirt are covered with chalk and oil
colors. His hair is all snaky with half-grown dreadlocks. He
doesn't look like a hatchet murderer anymore. He just looks
like a regular lunatic.

"Here," he says, shoving the picture at me.

It's the boy without a name. He's walking in a purple night on silver sand near a black ocean brightened by glowing white sea-foam. He's wearing jeans and a sweater, and he's holding a bag of red and white striped candy that glows like the sea-foam, and he's trailing a stick behind him, lazy. His legs and middle are sort of hard to see, but his shoulders and neck are a little clearer, because he disappears from the bottom up, and his light brown face and black baseball cap with the orange X and the gold ball earring and his squint smirk are clear as day.

"You got his eyes wrong," I hear myself say to Eric, who shrugs and lights up a blunt.

Mickey pads over to the bathroom to see. He looks carefully, while I hold the picture out for him and lean hard against the sink.

"It nice," he tells Eric. Then he stares up at me, all eyes and worry lines. "Why you crying?"

"I'm not," I argue, my voice high and melting, my insides all unfrozen.

"Why she lie?" Mickey asks Eric.

Eric moves into their room, opens the window, and flops back on their bed.

"Don't worry about it none," he tells Mickey. "Girls is crazy."

Turn the page for a preview of *Dime*, another astounding and gritty novel from E. R. Frank.

WHEN I FIRST understood what I was going to do, I expected to write the note as Lollipop. But in the six weeks since then, I've had to face facts. Lollipop has lived in front of one screen or another her whole life, possesses the vocabulary of a four-year-old, can't read, and thinks a cheeseburger and a new pair of glitter panties are things to get excited about. Using her is just a poor idea.

Back in August, Daddy assigned Lollipop to me, saying, *You school her.* I must have been doing a good job hiding my insides from him, or he wouldn't have. L.A. was still the only one of us who was allowed to touch the money. If she found out, it would be the second time she'd learn about Daddy asking me to hold coins. Which would only make things worse than they already were.

Lollipop didn't know the difference between a twenty and a one. "What's that?" She held out her hands, nails trimmed neatly and painted little-girl pink. She was polite, even if she was stupid. "May I touch it, please?"

"Nobody touches the money but Daddy."

"Listen to you," Brandy said from the couch where she was dabbing Polysporin on the cut over her eye that was taking so long to heal. "Cat gave back your tongue?"

"You're touching the money now," Lollipop said. She leaned her head in close to get the best look she could. Then she sniffed. At the one first. Then the twenty. "It stinks."

"Stop," I told her. "Money is dirty. You don't know where it's been. Don't put your nose on it."

Brandy grunted. "That there the funniest thing I heard all week." She didn't sound amused.

I pointed. "That's a two." I pointed again. "That's a zero. That's twenty."

"I know that says twenty." Lollipop pretended to be offended. She was obviously lying. "What's that one?"

"A one next to a zero is ten. You didn't even learn any of this from TV?"

"They have numbers on *Sesame Street* all the time," Lollipop said. "And *Little Einsteins*. *Mickey Mouse Clubhouse*. They have it on a bunch of stuff. So I know them, but I never paid attention to what's more. Only I know a hundred is a lot and a thousand is even more than that. A thousand keeps me pretty in pink."

"Do you know letters?" I asked.

Lollipop nodded. "Yeah," she said. "TV and Uncle Ray taught me those."

Brandy grunted again. "I bet he did."

"Do you know how to read?"

"Some signs." Lollipop scrunched up her face, thinking. *"Exit."*

I waited.

"Ladies. Um. *Ice."*

I waited some more.

"Maybe that's all the signs I know. But I can read two books."

That didn't seem likely. "Which ones?"

"'In the great green room, there was a telephone and a red balloon . . .'"

Some kind of a hiss or a gasp or the sound of a punctured lung came out of Brandy.

"'. . . and a picture of the cow jumping over the moon.'"

Brandy flew off the couch as much as anybody still limping can and smacked Lollipop so hard that Lollipop fell, a perfect handprint seeping onto her cheek. She didn't cry out a sound.

Not a whimper, not a squeak. She just got still, like a statue knocked over. You have to respect an eleven-year-old who gets smacked like that for no good reason and keeps quiet. That Uncle Ray trained her well.

"Brandy!" I stepped between the two of them. Brandy wasn't weak, but this. This was a whole side of her I never knew existed.

Her face was twisted up again the way it had been the other day with Daddy, only now it was beat up from him, fat lip and bruised eyes.

"What was that?" Brandy asked Lollipop. Her cut seeped blood right through the shiny Polysporin. "What was that?"

Lollipop answered as plain as she could manage. She didn't move any part of herself but her mouth. "*Goodnight Moon.*"

"Get off the floor."

"Brandy." Those flames that were lit in my belly the day we took Lollipop rose up, flaring. Was Brandy going to turn vicious now, on top of everything with Daddy? But Lollipop was standing, calm as anything.

"Don't you ever say those words again." Brandy smacked Lollipop's other cheek. Lollipop went down. This time tears oozed like rain dribbling down a wall.

"Daddy's going to kill you," I told Brandy. Even saying

Daddy made me want to slide through the floor and die, but there was nowhere to slide to and no way to die, so somehow I just kept on.

Brandy slipped around the corner to the alcove where my sleeping bag was. I heard her zipping into it. *L.A.'s going to kill you!* I wanted to shout, but the cat took back my tongue again. Anyway, probably Daddy was getting home before L.A., who was doing an outcall. So Daddy would get to Brandy first.

I hauled Lollipop up and propped her on the couch. I made sure the bills we had been studying were in my back pocket. Then I wrapped ice in a paper towel and held it to both sides of her face. She had white features and good, light-brown hair. Her skin was the color of wet sand. Mostly she seemed white, but with that color, it was confusing. She was prettier than the rest of us. Baby-faced.

"What's the other book you know?" I asked her. "Whisper." I didn't want Brandy hearing anything else that might make her charge back out here. But it had been a long time since anybody could talk to me about any kind of book.

"'Be still,'" Lollipop whispered. "It's monsters. There's more, but I can't remember it right now."

Somebody who smelled like barbecue potato chips used to cuddle me on her lap and read to me. I didn't remember the reader; just that salty, smoky scent and something scratchy on my left shoulder every time a page was turned. I remembered the books, though: *Goodnight Moon* and *The Snowy Day*.

"'A wild ruckus,'" Lollipop tried.

"Rumpus." I used to love *Where the Wild Things Are*.

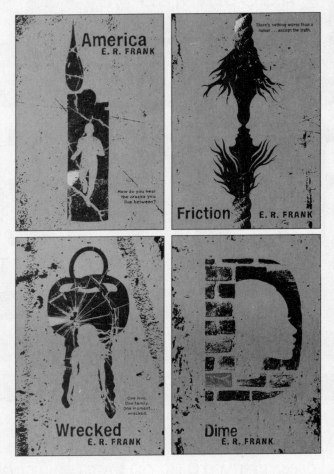

CHECK OUT THESE GRIPPING STORIES FROM ACCLAIMED AUTHOR

JASON REYNOLDS

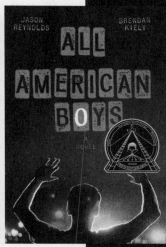

"An unexpectedly gorgeous meditation on the meaning of family, the power of friendship, and the value of loyalty."
—*Booklist* on *When I Was the Greatest*

"A vivid, satisfying, and ultimately upbeat tale of grief, redemption, and grace."—*Kirkus Reviews* on *The Boy in the Black Suit*

★"Timely and powerful, this novel promises to have an impact long after the pages stop turning."
—*School Library Journal*, on *All American Boys*, starred review

PRINT AND EBOOK EDITIONS AVAILABLE
atheneum simonandschuster.com/teen

  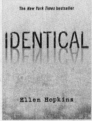  

19 foster parents,
23 attorneys,
and 44 caseworkers.

In this inspiring true story of Ashley Rhodes-Courter's life in foster care, she fights against the prejudices of her classmates, an abusive foster family, and a flawed system with hopefulness and endless courage.

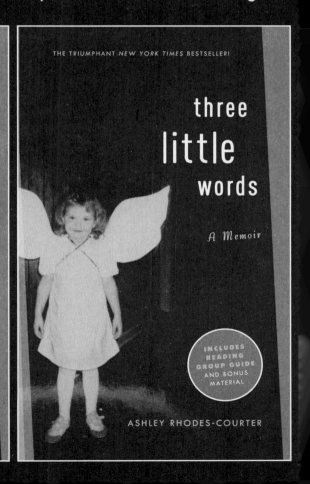